Perdita

ISBN-9798716968905

Printed in the United States of America
First edition 2021

"Where you come from is gone, where you thought you were going to never was there, and where you are is no good unless you can get away from it."

~ Flannery O'Connor

Chapter One

Seo-Yu Lee was not one to consider herself lucky. Seo-Yu was an only child, and led a loner's life all throughout elementary and middle school. That life pursued Seo longer than intended. As a junior in high school, she felt worse off than before, and she did not feel optimistic for the future. The feeling intensified because of her parents' recent absence.

The last time Seo-Yu saw her parents was at the airport, during their departure for a business trip. Her parents' destination was halfway across the country. The flight lasted two hours. Seo received a phone call from them, before they went to bed. The call was quick; a simple announcement they were going to bed, that they would be home by the end of the week, and an instinctive "Love you" from Seo-Yu's mom.

Twenty-four hours after the Lee parents' good night phone call, a city-wide lock-down was put in place. Seo needed to stay in her family's apartment until the lock-down lifted. Though nervous, she decided not to call her parents back - *maybe there is a riot going on over some sports game.* That would be no reason to call. *This will be over soon.*

The lock-down never ended, and instead turned into a quarantine. The transformation of public treatment was only the first odd occurrence. Seo-Yu never heard from her parents again, and the only other family Seo had any contact with for the first days of lock-down was her Aunt on her dad's side. Rachel was unhelpful, but at least a living person's voice to hear, who responded and conversed with her niece real-time. July turned into August, and when looking back... five weeks elapsed faster than any time ever had to the young girl.

Seo-Yu was sitting on the couch, when she leaned back and closed her eyes, letting herself take in the strange change of events that transpired in the past few weeks starting with the lock-down.

No one out after 11:00 p.m. or before 5:00 a.m. The Lee's was not the only city that went into a flat-out quarantine.

There was no more unnecessary travel out of state, as all the big cities bought into typical lock-down measures. The travel economy reduced to naught, and affordable airports and airlines took a financial hit. A sickness was going about, and many areas were sounding a figurative alarm. No need for the real one, yet. That type of sound would send Seo out of her mind.

Seo-Yu's thinking time became unusable due to the sirens. Any silence she was blessed with was often squandered with worry. The internet did not work anymore, so she could not keep track of the exact numbers. Seo-Yu wanted to see the numbers so bad, but could only imagine how they skyrocketed since her last look. Seo never bothered checking in on the numbers for the rest of the world, back when she *could* use the internet.

Seo-Yu regretted that stage of not caring. The numbers were another thing she wanted to know, right after she had no access to the website that stored them.

The last time Seo looked, the U.S.A. was leveling 200,000 deaths. She assumed the rest of the world could only be as bad.

What was relevant to the American teen was her country, her state, and above all else, her city. The United States of America let everybody on the continent down. *There are worse places to live, though.* New York City or San Francisco would be hell holes, with so many people stacked on top of each other. Seo's parents were in neither city, but Austin was not small compared to her city.

Lee's parents were set to return two days and 20 hours after lockdown went into effect. By then, there were fewer commuters on the streets, and Seo-Yu saw less people coming home to or leaving any of the three buildings in the complex. The absence of traffic in and out throughout the day was not normal. No airport taxis pulled over, either on the front or the side of the apartment building. Building A.

Seo kept an ear on the lookout, but no key ever so much as tapped the lock on her family's door. Number 22. Seo-Yu and her family lived in apartment A22. Seo could see down the front of the building, and from another room, one of the side roads. She had to go out to the main hallway to see the south side.

No sign of Mom and Dad. Seo-Yu lost hope that her parents would come home after some days of absence, considering her parents never came home any other way than by car. Seo tried to distract herself from their disappearance, but parents were a noticeable asset in any minor's life. *Less people are willing to drive these days. Maybe the bus is the next best bet.*

There was still that little bit of hope, and a bus stop five blocks down. Not that the Lees would ever make use of that. On day three of lock-down, Seo-Yu found that the common nomenclature people used turned from lock-down to quarantine. *Quarantine. Quarantine.*

We're in quarantine. Quarantine everywhere. The teenager was left on her own, with the contents of the three bedroom apartment. News channels were one of the few ways Seo-Yu could see the real world. Within the first week of her forced independence, the news she watched for multiple hours a day was the one to announce the suspect.

The whole of America was facing a virus under the name of Perdita. Besides Seo's missing parents, everything seemed routine to her, during that first week the virus infiltrated the country. Seo-Yu's friends were still on their Vegas trips and the world did not slow. Perdita had not reached her, yet. Not long after that hectic week was over, every state fell victim, and the world did slow - unlike past epidemics, there were no safe zones, outside of rural areas.

Going up in the mountains or out in the desert preserved a person from a communicable disease like Perdita, but most modern humans were not primed for that life. Seo was one of the many, her life skills geared toward surviving the concrete jungle before a real one. Not that Cedar City was very city-like, but Seo-Yu lived a life with few interactions with a rural livelihood. Even before her move, the place she saw animals was at the zoo. There was so much empty land, but the entire area was not good for farms and hunting, blamed on the freeway and outlying unincorporated towns.

Seo-Yu Lee remembered having the thought when the virus first hit her area, that Montana would be a good place to move to. Seo-Yu never finished the formation of that thought. There was no way for her to get there, and nowhere for her to stay if she did. Montana stayed a thought, and nothing more. Seo lazed around on the pleather couch, glued to her TV.

On one hand, the contraction rate of Perdita was significant enough for the news programs to talk about the virus as their headliners. On the other, more political hand, multiple news platforms said the illness was like a fever, and a few people were having a bad reaction to the effects. Seo-Yu knew which ones to listen to, but the amount of mixed messages was enough to drive people insane. Some other people did not know what to follow. Seo was not one for social media, but she saw people's state of mind whenever she hopped online.

The ensuing insanity both pushed Seo-Yu away, and drew her back in. Disgust was the driving factor. Someone must have put down a ramp in the wrong place, and at the wrong time. There was no other way to explain the explosion of cases, hospitalizations, and deaths. Going outside was no longer safe, once the crazies escaped the realm of the internet.

Seo watched the numbers on the CDC website flick upward, as they did every single day at 12:00 p.m. There were never any actual downturns, when looking at the nation as a whole. The original, minimal damage multiplied to hundreds of thousands of people dead, millions on their way to the same end. In the wake of the devastation, the news publicized anarchy.

In contrast, Seo-Yu did not see too much ravaging in real life. The destruction of her city was gradual, never brought to extremes. Some broken windows and a few tags from gang-wannabes. No bombs or mass shootings. Two months in, and Cedar City looked like everybody in a 50 mile radius disappeared.

Ripped flags flapping in the breeze and empty cars which sat in parking spots occupied for weeks on end were Seo-Yu Lee's most consistent company. The inanimate objects stayed longer than the birds flying overhead. She was not the only one who stayed indoors as much as possible, but she was also among the few. Seo-Yu was not willing to risk contamination from strangers, or her neighbors. Seo did not mind spending days at a time in voluntary solitude, however boring those days became.

The teen ate vegetables and bread and cereal until the pantry ran out, or the food grew stale and moldy. By that time canned food was all there was left to eat, and that grew old in a different way. Seo-Yu hated beans. On the third week, she had a bigger problem than black, brown, baked, or green beans to worry about. Irrigation went down, and culinary water ran out fast.

The taps ran dry and the food fizzled out, once and for all. No more sprinklers watering lawns. The grass died. Seo resorted to drinking what was left in her family's apartment. That included a bottle of white wine.

Seo-Yu's parents never touched alcohol. That thing was old - probably only kept around for parties' sake. She did not think on the forehand to save the orange juice for mixing in, before starting into the bottle. Through desperation, there was at least one night where Seo-Yu Lee was drunk. On top of the nasty taste of the stuff, hangovers did not prove to be a fun experience.

Seo-Yu also knew she could not last off of one now-emptied bottle of alcohol, forever. The teen's nerves were at a high, as the time came for her to leave the safety of the apartment, and find supplies to survive on. Seo-Yu shook out her nerves, trying to work up the courage to leave the safety of the home she lived in for the last four years. The preparation was more nerve-wracking than Seo expected. She knew right off the bat there was the possibility she might not come back to have a night of sound sleep in her own bed, but she did not know what else to prepare for.

The newly independent teenager decided to stick to her decision, and pushed her mind and body past her usual casual disposition. Seo put herself out the door and onto the gray-carpeted path to the outside. Seo-Yu started her quest off by first not going all the way out of the building. She investigated the apartment's leasing office, which was on the main floor of building A. The environment was different enough.

B and C were separate entities, though enlisted under the same company. Seo pressed the button on the front of the drinking fountain. The spout dribbled, and the teen caught a couple drops, but there was no more water running through the pipes. *The mini-fridge.* The little 2x2 refrigerator held complimentary drinks for visitors!

Seo realized the mini-fridge was in the lobby the entire time she was too afraid to leave her apartment, and she kicked herself for not thinking of that possibility earlier. Seo-Yu marched across the dim lobby to the dirty white miniature fridge, her mood bolstered. The dingy color glowed against the dark background. Seo ripped open the small door, the sound of something sticky catching her attention before anything inside caught her eye. The fridge was no longer cold.

What the confident high schooler found within was disappointing. There was no plethora of food and water waiting for Seo to feast upon. All she saw was a plastic grocery store bag, and sitting behind that, a mini water bottle and a can of ordinary soda. Upon further inspection, the bag held a bunch of oranges, most old and riddled with mold. The oranges looked gross, but Seo-Yu did her best to ignore the grossness.

Seo picked out the least mold-covered of the three, holding them as tenderly as she could manage to not cause further bruising. Seo-Yu stuck her thumb nail through the skin, and peeled a chunk away. A little juice popped out. Outside would show a different story, but in the dark, the inside looked edible. *Okay.*

Seo kept the open orange for her lunch, and snatched up the miniature water and the can of soda. Better to drink later than not at all. She did not have a full cart, but a little bit longer of sustenance was enough. And within a day, Seo-Yu had nothing left to eat, again. She wandered her building, putting off what she knew she needed to do.

Passing time was an endeavor, anyways. *I know I need to leave, I know, I know, I know. I just can't.* The bored teenager worked up the nerve to try doors, as she wandered. Seo-Yu was only seventeen, but she was far from the naive little girl that many adults saw her as.

Seo considered that people were hiding away in a lot of the apartments, so she stayed cautious, putting her ear to doors before trying their handles. Seo-Yu knew she tugged at some handles with people behind them, but nobody confronted her, so she was left to continue her walk in the realm of the living. Seo-Yu Lee did happen upon one other unlocked door not far from hers, also located on the second floor. Seo-Yu took a peek, before feeling comfortable enough to step all the way in. The two bedroom space was empty of people.

Behind the pantry and fridge doors, Seo found the apartment was already cleared out of food. She took the opportunity to instead grab clothes out of one of the closets. Never hurt to have more. Seo-Yu could not expect to have heating in the winter, anymore. Back in the apartment's kitchen, she fetched a green plastic cup, and emptied out whatever water was left in both the bathroom and kitchen taps.

All warm water. After Seo drank the bit of water and sat back in her own home for a little while, she decided there was no more appropriate time to leave the apartment building. Seo-Yu grabbed a kitchen knife, and went on an investigation of the surrounding buildings. A couple more rooms crossed off the list. She found that food and water were not hard to come by; all she had to do was be careful while searching.

Seo braced herself for what was to come. Listening was the key. Any store or apartment she entered could house someone who would not hesitate to kill her. There could be a stranger lost to the Perdita virus, who would try to spread their sickness one step further. When life was good, that was not the case.

Life was not good anymore. *Sitting in a classroom learning about transcendentalism would be so much better for me right now.* In previous years, Seo-Yu never thought she would miss going to school. Weeks after summer break ended and school would start again, she found she yearned for the back to school season. The idea was so strong in Seo's head that she made an audible grunt.

That was too much noise. Seo-Yu assumed her forced quiet state again. The infecteds' sole intention was feeling any living thing's warmth, especially humans, which was a more sinister implication than one would think, upon introduction. The heavy nature of the implication was motivation enough for Seo to live her new life as careful as possible. Seo-Yu turned out good at staying quiet, and at outrunning the people who gave chase to her, in those first few days on the wild city streets.

The infected were not slow by any means, but on a good note, they *were* clumsy and blind. They tripped on any obstacles in their path, and Seo created a few more of those obstacles, for safekeeping. She learned how to climb various fences and gates, and in the process traversed areas she was not familiar with, for the sake of familiarizing herself with her city. On the same route, Seo-Yu decided her best bet was to avoid alleyways and underground places, where there was a possibility of something or someone cornering her. Seo did not need any education on avoiding contact with the multitude of dead bodies surrounding the hospital.

Seo-Yu spent little time learning the importance of checking rooms before entering, as that was also a necessary precaution. As the weeks passed, she learned where in the city to go, and how and where to light fires, to lure the infected away. Most of all that Seo-Yu Lee learned, she learned silence. Seo-Yu would talk to herself, or to inanimate objects, but besides those instances of attempting to keep her sanity, silence became her most consistent routine. A routine was a necessary factor of life.

Considering the new world order, Seo needed to follow a routine now more than ever. She took time to organize everything she needed to survive life alone, and found the order all those things needed to stay in, for her to thrive. For two full weeks, Seo-Yu's routine worked, but her measures were not enough. The long term altered the dynamic Seo had set up - every time she opened the freezer door there was less food, and she had to throw out as much as she ate, as time went. Seo-Yu needed to last longer than two weeks.

The past months showed that the universe was not one for consistency. In the same non-pattern, a new hurtle appeared in Seo's path. She set her schedule up every week so that Wednesdays and Saturdays were grocery days - that worked best. Seo-Yu's trips to the store held complications aplenty, and she was not keen on taking multiple trips in one day.

Seo expected that every trip would hold as much stress as the last, and would not be worth the effort, leaving her with a hoard of untouched food sitting in her kitchen. The young woman would become a city-wide target, if all the food disappeared at once. People would track Seo down so fast. She was not smart enough. Seo-Yu could not take that risk.

Gathering food over time would suffice. Seo missed the times that she rode bikes down to the store with her dad to pick up food for the week. That was one of the few times Seo-Yu spent time with her father. Regrettable. Both of Seo's parents' work schedules were always full.

Seo-Yu talked with her mother more than her father, but even that mother-daughter relationship was all but nonexistent. Productive activities were the only times Seo interacted with them for more than a few minutes at a time, once she reached the sixth grade. Now Seo-Yu, who was a part of the loner lifestyle in the first place, could not interact at all. That road only led to suffering. Seo-Yu Lee never knew what she missed out on.

Seo-Yu found herself alone in the same Walmart she always went to, since her family's move to Cedar City. The reminder was a pest. Seo considered any reminder of old life a pest.

She tried not to think about that topic much. After two weeks of fishing around, the store was starting to run out of some necessary supplies.

Seo-Yu never saw anyone else in the store, but most of the food did not get a chance to rot before disappearing, as she noticed by the time she started to shop on her own. Things like milk and some less desirable fruits stunk up the place, but meat and vegetables and cheeses were emptied out. So many empty boxes and stands. Seo still managed to find what she needed during the past couple of weeks, and this time was no different, though pickings were slimming out. Seo-Yu searched out the basics things she needed. It got to the point that she used garden gloves to keep her bare hands clean from any bad germs.

Seo-Yu Lee found most of what she needed, like usual. Seo-Yu wished to herself that the store had an automatic Replenish setting that she would stumble upon one day, preferable to be in the near future. That was still a ridiculous notion. A thought limited to the imagination. *I'll have to move on to a new store, one day.*

Seo thought of other grocery store options. The Smith's on Red Rock was farther than the Walmart, but the next closest grocery store to her. *I need to check that out soon,* Seo-Yu thought. She focused back on her current task. While the teenager was in the process of surveying the candy aisle, the store intercom turned on.

Two dings. No voice followed, but the tone was enough to startle Seo-Yu. As the speakers turned on, she dropped a half-full grocery bag on top of her foot, startling herself double. There were a couple human throat-ish noises from other aisles, in response to the sound that rang over the speakers. That brought Seo's heart rate up, and she put the crinkly bag inside of her backpack.

Seo-Yu was not the only one put on high alert. The store came alive. The ding and rustling bag were loud enough to draw the infected away from whatever they were paying attention to before. Seo heard multiple en route to areas of the store with speakers overhead. Time was ticking.

Who pressed the button? Seo-Yu's brain hissed right back at herself, as if she were speaking to another person. Seo's thoughts only bounced back to herself. *Now I might be found.* Seo-Yu's heart pumped hard as she listened to their movements around the store. She thought her own heart would beat right out of her chest.

Seo tried to work out what to do, but she did not have enough time to put together a full plan. Three far-gone and already decaying infected appeared at one end of the aisle. Seo-Yu turned around, and was glad to see the way she came in was clear. For the time being. Seo needed to take the chance.

She picked up speed and broke through the end of the aisle in time to miss another runner, who was only hindered by an inability to locate her. The monster did not turn in Seo-Yu's direction until too late to change the direction he was going. She watched long enough to see him run into a wall. There was no give in the popcorn texture, and there ensued an audible thump as the dying body made impact on the hard, vertical surface. That "person" may have broken some bones.

That would be good news. *More of them should do that.* None of the four forgot that Seo was there, and they pursued with fervor, stomping over bags and small objects, creating more noise all the while. The running caused two more to show their faces, at the far end of the store. They were not a huge worry, as they were farther away.

Only a few more infected packing on to the others to worry about. Seo-Yu could not help but wonder how she was not found out fifteen minutes earlier. The answer was easy: Seo was lucky. As far as she could see, the door out was not blocked by attacking bodies. Seo-Yu was almost out of the store!

Then, there was a moment that ruined all of her progress. One step that Seo did not take a proper look at, to see where her foot was going. Seo-Yu's foot hit the ground in a usual running motion, but instead of hitting hard flooring, there was a sharp slap as her foot connected, and she slipped. The pool of blood pulled Seo-Yu Lee down onto the slick floor. Her hands and then torso slapped down hard on the laminate floor, the impact releasing an involuntary groan out of her mouth, like all the air rushing out of a balloon.

Seo-Yu's head was inches from hitting the self-checkout cashier stand. *Get up, get up, get up!* She was frantic. Seo managed to stumble up, wiping her hands on her jeans. Seo-Yu's eyelashes prevented her from using her entire field of vision.

They were heavy with thick, red liquid. But, Seo was still in a physical state to run, and that was all that mattered to her. The teenager sped along, not giving the fall any further thought, as she was already taken up by a dangerous situation. *Don't die.* Seo only rubbed her eyes clear well after she resumed her run.

Blood soaked Seo-Yu's gloves, and she slid them off and threw them behind her, distracting one runner. The whole chase lasted minutes, but felt like hours as the monsters ate up the distance between themselves and the one living being who was *almost* within their reach. Every step was crucial. Sight was Seo's only boost in the situation. Her backpack bounced up and down on her back - the feeling was annoying, but necessary.

Having the backpack was important. Seo-Yu did not want to drop the bag, and at the same time ensure somebody else would find her next few days' worth of meals. Seo was glad she was not carting soda cans around, this time. They would be undrinkable, by now. Cans alone would bang against each other and create noise, so Seo-Yu had the foresight as far back as a week ago to put towels in between such loud containers.

Seo's mind proved dependable in distracting her, at any time - even while running was not out of the question. Seo-Yu thought of an even worse situation: heavier, metal-cased foods, like canned vegetables. That would hurt even more than thin aluminum and fizzing liquid knocking in Seo's ears. She received a whole batch of luck, not for the first time in her life, and survived along with her scavenged food to see another day. And a second day.

And a third. Saturday. The Lee's apartment was seven blocks from the city center, and the whole area – a lot of suburban life, though also business oriented - was always a safe place. Seo-Yu and her family never had any problems the entire time they lived at the Mayflower. Not that Seo's parents took time to enjoy the place.

Her route was advantageous enough to put pursuing monsters behind, but not at seeing a person like herself. A wooden board propped three inches off the ground here, a car tire over there, whatever they could trip on or run into.

Die over. Being a Saturday, the time for Seo-Yu's next trip to the grocery store arrived. The walk to the store was safe.

Seo brought along her almost empty backpack - only the usual contents of two lighters, a permanent marker, and a paper towel accompanied her there. Seo-Yu was becoming used to the walk, to the point where she did not feel winded, or even exercised anymore. *I should start biking this again.* Biking would at least work different muscles, which Seo knew she had not put to use in a long while. Seo-Yu's only problem with bicycles was the added noise, and the fact that she could not carry extra bags on the ride home.

Since Seo only needed to provide food for herself, she could use her backpack to carry everything. No need for separate bags. A backpack would work on top of a bike. There were multiple times in recent weeks Seo-Yu ran all the way home, for one reason or another. For a number of years before, she rode her bike to and from the store.

I need to start using my bike again.
Anxious to wrap the job up, Seo A-lined between a pair of the self-checkout cash registers. That was when something gross on the ground in front of Seo-Yu caught her eye, the sight jarring enough to stop her in her tracks. Seo's brain left numerous topics in the dust, to focus on one big one. As she stared down at the same blood puddle she slipped in while on the run on Wednesday, the memory of what happened in that moment resurfaced, clear as day.

That was on Wednesday. There were multiple sets of dried blood footprints all muddled together, heading out of the checkout lane, and in the direction of the door. After that visit, Seo-Yu dropped her backpack at the door, washed her hands off as best she could, changed her clothes, and showered - as always, blood was disgusting. An idea dawned on Seo in the same moment she saw the brownish color and the sludgy make-up of the stuff. That blood was not innocent.

And worse than all else, there was nothing more that Seo-Yu worried about, on that night. The one time she let her guard down. Seo had her food. That was the last remarkable moment of the night. Reality was beginning to sink in.

The pool of blood was old, and looked like somebody spilled a container of mud on the floor. Seo did not need to run a test on the sludge. Nobody spilled mud. Though any person's blood gained a tough texture over time, she knew the source wound, and an inkling of the owner. The blood was not shed from a healthy person.

The make-up of the bodily fluid - congealed, and not so fluid anymore - was a direct point toward an infected culprit. The teenager only saw fresh-but-not-fresh blood like that, from them. A horrified feeling overtook her. Seo committed one of the worst sins in this day and age, by touching that blood. She may have been fine if there was nothing chasing her, in the first place.

If Seo-Yu had the time to jump in a swimming pool, clean her eyes, then scrub herself with soap, and soak again. Seo regretted not setting the grocery store on fire. Not that that would have had a good ending. Who knew if the flames would have even caught in the first place? Seo-Yu tried to quantify the problem in her head.

That did not get Seo any further. Over the past seven days, she had grown certain that she was the only one who used the Walmart in the morning. Seo-Yu knew, by the systemic way she placed cans or bags on the ground, and along the shelves. No items a typical person would move, ever moved. That prompted one morbid idea to stretch, and push all others out of the way.

Time was closing in, and Seo managed to waste the past two days away. *Goddamn fantastic.* The sarcasm sounded strong in her head. Nobody else would have heard if Seo-Yu said something out loud, but she kept the words to herself, in case. Seo took extra care while rummaging through what junk food was left in the ever emptying grocery store.

Seo-Yu was wary, but frustrated. Frustration was an understandable reaction to what occurred during the last visit. The last time may have cleared out the infected, but one never knew until they completed a full sweep of the building. Seo took the rest of the canned food home two trips ago. Marshmallows, less desirable candy, and frozen meals (all of which were encased in soggy boxes and far from frozen anymore) that looked safe were Seo-Yu's best bets.

All non-food products like paper, kitchenware and hygiene were gone before the first day of the next month. By the time Seo was ready to head home, she did not expect any more infected to be in the store, as she had not heard any sounds besides those that came from her. The fear from the last time pursued Seo-Yu. She was twice as scared and shaken, and the late bestowment of knowledge had her on the edge of a figurative cliff. Seo felt fine for the whole of Thursday morning, but as Sunday evening came on, symptoms started hurling themselves onto her denial.

Seo-Yu's vision started to blur. She did not realize what was happening at first, and wondered if she ate something bad. *Something must have gone really, really bad.* Seo knew from experience that bad food usually did not affect her eyesight in a negative way. She had had food poisoning before.

The puzzle pieces came together as the blur decided to stick around a while. Seo-Yu was looking through a thin layer of stained glass that never moved from in front of her face, no matter which direction she looked. Seo was now an official victim of the virus. *All the effort she had put in to get to this point, why for?*

Seo-Yu was at the end of her rope. *Deep breaths.* Those did not help heal anything. Seo took her moment to freak out, before a new thought surfaced to open air. That moment of the teenager's brain churning was the same moment she created a new plan.

Seo was about to end her suffering, once and for all. She did not have a desire to let her mind fade so far that she could not control herself. *I am not out to hurt people.* Seo-Yu did not have access to a gun, or any drugs that would act without causing her to suffer. She stared at the wall at what was likely a spider as it crawled from one side of the room to the next. Seo used to be deathly afraid of spiders. Now she thought about the fuzzy image the graced her vision as the only appropriate symbol of the trap she found herself in. The slow and unfortunate end she found herself about to face couldn't be any different than the way a fly feels as it struggles helplessly against the predator's web, with no choice but the accept its fate as it closes in.

She tried to think of a way out with an ending where she would be safe and sound, but not a single alternative surfaced. There were no clues buried anywhere; not even in the depths of

Seo-Yu's brain. She finally came to the conclusion that there was no happy solution waiting around the corner. There were no corners to wait behind. Contracting this virus was a one-track train.

Seo had a new responsibility on her plate: to remove any possibility of hurting other survivors, as there were few besides herself. Seo-Yu knew she was not the only one at the Mayflower. And there were others living spread throughout the city, too, who needed to stay preserved. Seo completed the climb up all the five flights of stairs built above her apartment, located in the medium-heighted apartment building. The hike took longer than expected, but at the end of the journey, Seo-Yu reached the point of throwing herself over the edge.

Seo towered over the street, boxy cars down below as small as her pinkie, and all of a sudden she became scared she would survive the fall, and she was also scared that she might not. *I can't do this. Nope. Can't.* Seo-Yu was not sure what state her body was in, but for all she knew, she was too far gone and a fall might not affect her enough to stop her from turning into a monster anyway.

I might end up paralyzed, and thirst to death down there. Like a flying bullet, the thought shot down the length of Seo's spine, in the form of a shiver. Discouraged by thinking, she returned to the stairwell door and pushed on the handle. The door did not budge. *What!*

No. Seo-Yu put her full weight on the door. No dice. Seo sighed, turned, and walked back to the edge of the building, taking another look down. She realized the universe was telling her something, as she looked over the edge.

The rest of the world spiraled down below Seo-Yu. *Or not. The universe isn't telling me shit. That's just my brain. My stupid, probably beginning to decay, brain.* She turned away from the ledge for a second time. Back to the stairwell door. Seo-Yu Lee gave another push.

Seo-Yu found the door's attitude did not change during that one minute she stepped

away to the middle of the rooftop getaway.
Tears further obscured Seo's vision, which was
already made poor by sickness. *I am never
going to get off this building this way. What luck?*
Seo-Yu fiddled with the top and bottom of the
door handle.

Finding no new outcome, she bent down
and put her eye up close to the wavy knob,
which helped reduce the blur effect. Seo did not
have a need to be on the roof often, and did not
know the go-around for getting back into the
stairwell. She stayed stationed at the door, trying
to tell if there was some kind of key lock, or
some other unlocking button she was failing to
see. Seo-Yu pushed and pushed and pulled. All
of a sudden, the door opened towards her, and
she all but fell over backwards with the motion,
the opening door stubbing her toe.

The frazzled teenager tried not to worry
about if she still had the toe nail intact or not.
This was not the time to worry about such
things. Seo-Yu had only pushed on the handle
for the last four minutes, when she instead

needed to pull. *I am starting to lose my mind.* Seo stumbled back down the way she came.

Shapes helped Seo-Yu move about. Doorways sunken into walls and knee-heighted trash cans sitting outside of the same doorways were easy to notice, even with limited vision. But the path down was blurry. Seo-Yu Lee felt comfortable in the thought that she would always get home, no matter the situation, as long as she did not make any mistakes along the way. Seo-Yu knew her own apartment number, so she double-tasked, using her travel time to make sure she was safe, while counting her way home.

Seo was successful in finding the correct apartment, helped by knowing what floor to stop at and how far down the hallway her apartment was. Seo-Yu felt that was necessary information for when she lost her vision, later on. Losing vision was an inevitable part of the infection. That fact depressed Seo further. She closed the door and searched out a clear spot on the ground where she could flop down and cry the rest of her eyesight out.

Tears would make seeing an even harder task, but there was no reason for Seo-Yu not to speed up the process, when she was already taken up by so many other problems. Seo sat around thinking about death, destruction, what the world had come too. She let her train run until she focused back in and realized that the apartment was too dark to see in. The lights were out, Seo-Yu could hardly see, and her mind matched the state of the lighting. She pushed herself up to a standing position, once she assured herself she was good to move.

Instead of doing something productive, Seo once again wanted to attempt suicide. She went a different route from jumping off of a building. Seo-Yu reached out, and flipped on the nearest of the pre-placed flashlights to provide some needed guidance. Seo shuffled around and got hold of a pinkish rope, meant for securing tarps to trailer beds, and the like. That was what she planned to use to hang herself.

Seo-Yu started by tying the rope around the top portion of one of her bunk bed posts. By the time Seo started her personal execution, she learned the post would not do the job she expected. Seo-Yu was too tall. Probably the first time that had ever been a problem. Her toes were able to touch the floor if she stretched far enough, and touching the floor was seventeen years too natural.

Those six seconds of realization during strangulation were enough for Seo to stop wanting to try dying again, at least by hanging. Jumping off of a building was also outside of her abilities, as proved a mere two hours earlier. There was only one way to go, and that was the direction Seo-Yu was already going in. In a downward spiral. She continued on the path to blindness - she was an unwilling candidate, but forced to comply.

The demands were heavy. Pain was pervasive, and that did Seo in. She did not want to feel what the rest of her conscious time would present. Seo-Yu's moods were all over the board. In the mornings she would be alert and working to figure out new aspects of blindness, and in the afternoon, have a relapse into suicidal ideation.

Seo figured slitting her throat would do the trick. There was no reason for Seo-Yu to follow her first inclination of cleanliness, any more - committing to action a third time, as she still saw death as her only way out. Seo knew where the kitchen was by years of memory, and exited the spare bedroom to reach her new goal. The door was open this time; no need to fret about spending valuable time searching for the spherical, slippery handle.

Seo-Yu's mind was a blur, which jammed up her regular, speedy thought processes and prevented her from thinking as she usually would. Seo reached the kitchen counter after much suspense, and was unable to find a good knife right off the bat. She knew they were all in the utensils drawer, which was somewhere, but her hand landed at the junk drawer, instead. Inside the squeaky drawer Seo-Yu felt out multiple pens, and at that moment, a thought occurred to her. Seo changed her original plan.

Seo-Yu knew she could take the time to give people - strangers, all of them innocent - a warning. That was a productive task. Seo yanked open the front door, fighting back a wave of pain that washed through her forehead. One step beyond a continuous loss of eyesight were migraines, pelting Seo-Yu like a snowstorm. They did not last long, but they were there, posing a new and uninvited distraction.

Seo-Yu Lee tried to write down a well thought out warning, but since she could not see, she was not sure how legible or organized the writing was. There could be a big blob in place of an actual door, and Seo-Yu would be none the wiser. She gave up on writing, and threw her arm diagonally up and down twice, drawing an "X" on the bottom half of the door. That was a shape Seo did not need to see, to know. The hall lights shut off three days ago, or maybe four - she had no sense of passing time -

but even in the dark, if a newcomer had a flashlight, they would understand the X.

Seo-Yu trusted they would. She *knew* she was going to die, but one thought stayed consistent: she was not going to let other healthy people fall victim to her literal slip up, before she passed. Seo took what other aspects she could control into her own hands. Seo-Yu's highest priority was her focus on restraint. In the hopes of saving someone else, Seo resigned herself to staying in apartment A22 of the Mayflower, until she died.

Dying, like most people did after too long a period of starvation. At least there was a fair amount of space to rot away in, in peace. With how little the complex received looters in the past two months, Seo-Yu was sure nobody would find her. Seo still hated herself for failing to take action a full three days earlier. Right when the teenager was feeling comfortable in her routine, she failed to stay safe.

I wish I found people I knew, instead of staying alone when my family dropped off the face of the goddamned Earth. Seo did not realize how thirst and hunger would overtake her, when she first resigned herself to staying in her figurative tower. That all-encompassing thirst and hunger started to affect Seo-Yu when she was low, and overtook her faster than she prepared for. One step beyond no longer seeing, Seo felt an unprecedented cold overtake her. That was an odd feeling, even being at the tail end of summer.

Must have been the virus' doing. *The virus has not breached my thought process. Yet.* And by the textured bruises and dried-blood coated cuts Seo-Yu sustained over the Perdita affliction, she concluded she had not gained the tough skin of the infected. Seo-Yu Lee began to feel an extreme need for warmth, and that need linked up with the consistent cold sensation.

Seo-Yu was aware enough in the moment to remember that *this* was what the virus did to people. She had never seen the effects in person, and never in real time. Seo was seeing them now. To her, the real time happenings were part of a roller coaster that never dipped. Seo-Yu took the simple route, and wrapped herself up in a stack of blankets.

As the teenager huddled under the security of the stuffy covers that made her sweat, but not feel the effect of the multiplied heat, she noticed improvements to her hearing. A fly buzzed somewhere in the apartment. Not close by. Seo-Yu's senses of sight, touch, taste, and smell faded to the point she felt more alone than ever before. Only that fly was there, to unknowingly entertain Seo's hearing.

Not comforting at all. Other sounds appeared in the distance. She could tell that people were walking on the floor below hers, by her ears alone. That was surprising. Seo-Yu tipped herself over, to lay on her side, resting her head on the ground, ear pushed into the carpet, magnifying her hearing as much as she could manage.

Seo-Yu Lee heard a hint of footsteps come into earshot, and in that same moment she knew they were from the infected. Seo-Yu focused, using the opportunity to test her new level of hearing. Seo found herself wondering who the people were, before they turned. What a curious question, but a true one, that the short, skinny teenager desired an answer too. Each one of those things had a personality, maybe a family, and maybe a job. They had hobbies and friends and reasons to not be monsters. Now with their vision gone and their flesh rotting away; whether their brain is directly affected by the disease or not, they don't have much reason not to go mad.

Seo could not see any of the invaders, so she was not sure of the exact amounts of time - but she *was* certain they were farther along in the process than herself. There was nothing else for her to do with her time but *wonder* about things like that. Seo knew she had to keep thinking, or else the spiral into oblivion might do nothing other than accelerate.

Dynamic thinking was the best helper, but hard to accomplish. Seo-Yu kept on one track, thinking about how she would end up. It was a vicious cycle. Seo-Yu Lee switched her track of thought, after some inward effort. She listened to the infected feet as they dragged down on the main floor.

In the short lifetime before Seo-Yu went blind, she heard a lot of noises. Footsteps were one of them. The impact was clear back then, but to Seo's newest level of hearing, they were the poster child of clumsy. *I sound like that, don't I?* She knew that they were never rushed, until they heard a non-infected human.

And there was no rushing going on downstairs. That could only mean there were no true humans about. No humans making themselves known, at least. Seo-Yu still drew a conclusion. She did not count as a human.

Seo-Yu Lee did not need to wonder anymore if they laid off of other infected people like herself, even before they finished their mental deterioration process. Seo-Yu was witnessing the answer. On the other hand, she was not eager to search out the ones who were, at one time, her enemies. Witnessing that answer would not be as pleasant. The footsteps Seo heard became a consistent noise for what felt like a long while.

They were uneven and stumbling, and more infected began their investigation of the apartment building. At one point there were clearly a dozen. They contaminated a lot more surfaces in the process of their query. Most of the half-gone people went off on their own new opportunity, after a sweep of that floor. The non-infected humans were different, both in volume and mannerism.

Hopefully no new people touch all of that stuff the old ones touched. "That stuff" could be anything. Could be an unassuming trap for any passerby. That would be an absolute crying shame, for Seo-Yu to see more of her own go down such a bad path. She realized she did not need to worry about what things she touched anymore, at least in the interest of her own safety.

Seo-Yu Lee *did*, however, need to concern herself with the safety of other people, and the contamination of those people. That was, *if* Seo-Yu cared about their well-being enough to take on that responsibility in full. The responsibility was pure nature. Seo felt more and more apathetic about what might happen to other people, by the day. If the virus got into the healthy people's eyes or noses or mouths, they would turn, too.

That was how Seo-Yu turned. Blood sneaking into her mouth and nose and eyes. That moment was a death sentence. Seo scrunched her face and concentrated her mental efforts back on those people close by, who were not infected. Seo-Yu heard their soft, measured steps.

They *sounded* aware and cautious. Like Seo did. She never knew awareness had such a distinct sound. *Wow.* That was news.

A refreshing sight. *Sound. Whatever!* Seo was sure she sounded exactly like that, but divided by five, not more than four days ago. *How did I last so long like that?*

They're so easy to hear. Seo-Yu had so many related topics bouncing around in her head. From hours of pure thinking, a millionth new scenario grew from the ashes of Seo's company-deprived mind. She knew that if she had somebody in the room available to talk, she would stay as far from them as the apartment boundaries allowed. Seo-Yu did not need any temptations of the sort bothering her.

Seo lingered on the self-proposed situation. *What if somebody were here.* She made a point of convincing herself she would have the will to leave, if the not so probable case of somebody else being in the apartment did happen. Seo-Yu would escape to somewhere… certainly... and she would also need to avoid getting upset. Get as far away as possible, to keep the feeling of the need to attack at bay.

Or however all that worked. Seo assumed the described mentality came as natural as a feeling of sadness or thirst. That was the only line of action she could fathom. And Seo-Yu was feeling thirsty. *Urgh.*

Mind back to those yet untouched, who only stayed to check one apartment on the first floor of Seo's section of apartments, before moving on to the next worthless building. That one time Seo-Yu heard real people in the apartment building during her self-imposed quarantine was the first time she heard people she could infect, and her mind fixated. The state of her health was in shambles - she was teeter-tottering on the edge of a figurative cliff. That caused a butterfly effect of thoughts, and after some of that, Seo realized that she had not heard any more footsteps. Seo-Yu was the only one left in the building.

Seo knew she had to be on the edge of mental death, considering she was starting to think about infecting other people, and not in a negative manner. Seo-Yu trusted that when her mental death finally arrived, she would not feel the physical death coming for her soon after. Seo already felt enough pain. There were few visitors to the apartment building, posing no distraction to relieve the persistent feeling. She assumed there must have been an empty appearance to the place, to go along with the actual emptiness that surrounded her.

That is good protection. For the third time Seo-Yu focused back on the one and only set of visiting, living people. They stopped at the slightest of strange sounds, which even she could not make an interpretation of from her separate, self-imposed prison. Seo-Yu Lee stayed strong in her resolve, and did not so much as attempt to make contact during the fifteen or fewer minutes she heard the mumbles and feet of real people. If everybody else did the same thing, they might all come out of this virus safe.

These living humans down below moved in an even, purposeful manner. Seo-Yu was hopeful that they did not take any risks spreading possible infection. She supposed somebody was directing them, from the stage of a leader, by the sure sound of an organized crowd. Seo began to wonder why she had not heard all of those little differences earlier. *My hearing could not have improved that much.*

Maybe it's because I stayed away from any signs of life, since people started to die off. Seo-Yu trained her attention until she could no longer hear the people. Seo realized that they disappeared. That was a weird feeling - hearing them come, and then make their leave. Then came another migraine, to replace any previous mental productivity.

The migraines came when things were quiet, and hunger was what brought Seo-Yu out of the apartment. She was taught from a young age the importance of learning to navigate her home in the dark, though doing so while blind was tougher than instances with the lights off. Seo latched the front door closed behind her, in an attempt to make the hallway look yet undisturbed. Seo-Yu realized that the home she left stunk, even to someone hosting a diminished sense of smell. Seo used her outstretched hand to guide herself down the hallway, concrete and fabric getting the full up-down.

Seo-Yu did try a few doors as she went along, but the insides of most rooms were not accessible. Seo circled back around the other side of the wall for the sake of being thorough, and the second door on the same wall as her own surprised her. Whatever number that door was, was open. *Somebody must have been in here recently. Or it might be one of the apartments I've been in before.*

Seo-Yu could not remember the details of the neighbor's apartments that she visited on her previous rounds. Other than the one on Seo's own floor, and another on the bottom floor, there could be any number of reasons for the vacancy in this one. Seo-Yu stopped further progress, figuring she would brave investigation on a later date. Seo knew of the state of things in the current environment, and that she was safer not risking everything, and going back to her apartment. The fact that Seo-Yu left her house in the state she was in was already testy enough.

Seo-Yu Lee had a hard bite to chew in estimating the time as she crept around, but she assumed day time. Seo-Yu had always relied on clocks, and regretted not having the ability to rely on one now. She went back home for the night, but the next day (or, at least, after a period of sleep, which in most cases took up a night,) she mustered up the courage to leave. Seo closed the front door behind her again, found the elevator, and pressed a button. Seo-Yu was about to go farther than before, in the interest of finding water.

There was no ding when Seo-Yu Lee pressed the elevator down button, and no whir of doors sliding open. *Right.* The elevator did not work. Seo-Yu needed to use the stairs to get down to the bottom floor. She turned to the stairwell, took a deep breath, and started off in that direction.

Seo reached the end of the hallway and found she turned the wrong way in the first place, as there was no stairwell door in front of her, only a wall and a window. Seo-Yu did a 180 degree turn, following the wall and passing the elevator once again. The smooth metal was cold. Then fingers back to the wall, which was half fabric, and half concrete. The fabric was not as cold as the concrete.

The stairwell was equidistant from the elevator, as was the window Seo ended up at, first. The handle to the metal door was not as hard to utilize as she thought, even while blind, and neither were the stairs, however unnerving they were to traverse. Seo-Yu felt fresh air on her face at the same moment she opened the second metal door down, located on the main floor. Seo was not outside yet, but the standard door two feet to the right of the revolving one was open, propped up so by her, using a set of cinder blocks three weeks ago. No need for creaky hinges and wood slamming against more wood to ruin the day's work, by summoning the local beasts.

The Sun felt nice, only disappearing in certain areas, behind something big. That was not a new occurrence, but annoyed Seo-Yu. She tried to stay inside the rays of heat. The infected left Seo alone, making the streets safer overall for her to navigate, as a pedestrian. Seo-Yu kept to one side of the street the entire time she was out, and did not stray from walls, fences, or bushes.

Seo followed whichever kept her attached to the ground, limiting her travel to one almost straight path down the road. The artificial structures and natural growth crafted line was Seo-Yu's guide. She still had to worry about people, sidewalk hazards, and areas she did not know like the back of her hand. Not that Seo could see the back of her own hand. *I guess that idiom doesn't work anymore.* Not to mention, some of the hazards Seo-Yu placed earlier in the month were on their way back to bite her in the butt.

Karma, maybe. Not that Seo taking action to preserve her own life was malevolent. But the guilt was there, as the traps didn't discern whom they victimized. Seo-Yu knocked over some random objects, but did not encounter anything deadly, and nothing that inflicted pain. After the trip outdoors, Seo felt confident enough to travel around the block with a more productive end goal, for the next time.

Seo-Yu needed supplies. She figured her best choice was to search around the closer gas stations and smaller stores that may still hold chips, coffees, and items she skipped the first time around. Seo headed off. On the way, she learned to differentiate sounds, and not just the dramatic kinds, like a gun shot. Farther down the line, Seo-Yu learned to listen to and count the number of people - or not people - around her, by natural sound.

Seo heard more people than she did when back in the apartment, but meeting them was far beyond forbidden. Yet again, Seo-Yu missed the company of others. Hearing was her sole method of going about life. That was depressing. Listening could not tell Seo when she was about to walk into a sign post, or where a store was in reference to her location, but if somebody came at her, she was ready.

Seo-Yu did not know a better way to tell how close or far away people were standing, but by hearing, she could identify their speed when on the move. Whether they moved fast or slow was also an audible matter, and a skill for Seo to perfect over time. The first day she felt empowered was when she learned how to tell the time of day. The sound of birds marked the morning time. Seo-Yu spent that day in the park, with the purpose of learning how to work with animals.

Seo could not go to the store a mile away while blind, so why not find other resources closer? She could not count on wild animals as her main source of food, either, but she set up cardboard box traps in an attempt to catch the small ones. The teenager had not come close to having any authentic eating encounters with domestic animals. There were pets on the premises of the Mayflower, but considering she had not heard the pitter patter of paws in a few days, she assumed they died before she got desperate. Seo figured she would have eaten them by now, if they were alive.

Maybe I'll get lucky with these later, Seo-Yu thought of the boxes, as she left the overgrowing field. It didn't seem likely, but there were two noticeable tree roots Seo stepped upon on the way in, and she managed to go the same way out. The traps took up the entire day as far as Seo-Yu could gather, but she had all the time in the world to spend. Or more like a month of no eating. Or maybe one week of no water.

That would all feel like a long time in her current state. The only threat to Seo any longer were conscious humans, and her own self, that might waste away into oblivion in the middle of the city. Before Seo-Yu took her fall into the pool of blood, she ran from infected people, and gave living ones a wide berth. Seo's baseline of knowledge was that the infected were a danger.

Now Seo-Yu was one of them, meaning the game's switch flipped. The general infected roaming the street was no bother, but all uninfected assumed the status of threat - no cherry picking. Seo did not host the desire to chase them down yet, but they would kill her if they knew she was sick. They probably would, even if Seo-Yu was not stuck in sickness, but what she looked like would be the defining factor for many of those people. Seo had no idea what she looked like to outside eyes, but she could not expect a good response.

Seo-Yu could feel her hair sticking out in clumps and tufts, and she realized she never cared so little about the state of her hair. Seo's thoughts went so far as to hope she did not look approachable, as much as her natural self may have wanted to. Worse than meeting people and dying by gunshot, if they trusted Seo-Yu and she did not do anything to escape, they would touch her in some way, shape, or form. Then they would become infected too, and Seo doubted they would stay awake and alive for as long as she did. Seo-Yu thought about how she should have turned days ago; she doubted her interior timeline was that far off of real time, therefore her time on Earth should have ended.

Seo let her mind puzzle further. The innovator found the best places to hide herself, hoping she was not hidden somewhere visible, despite the fact that she spent a lot of her time out and about, rather than hiding in such places instead. Seo-Yu managed to stay out of other human being's ways. If she and everyone else still scouring the city stayed out of each other's way, everything would end up fine. All else aside, Seo knew through months of experience that not everybody followed that rule.

A lot of those people had guns. Too many were aggressive. *They're all too aggressive. That problem existed before the virus did.* The thought was not persisted. At the very least, the sickness did not affect Seo-Yu's personal views on the current, general populace.

With nothing physical to see, her memory came in full swing, but in a different format. With no true vision to distract her, the memoires seemed much more vivid than they used to. Seo could almost re-watch video clips, and re-look at pictures from old magazine articles. At least there were those memories, pictures in her head to distract from day-long boredom. They may not substitute for the memories Seo-Yu wanted, but they were there. She went over old things in her head, while walking about.

It wasn't like Seo could watch the clouds move about the sky or the trees shift. She followed a long stretch of rough cement on the side of a building down the street, until the wall dropped 90 degrees to her right. Seo-Yu's arm followed the abrupt angle, dropping off to the side, and the sharpness caused her to take a confused step backwards. Seo followed the new turn, however, and as she did, she heard the grind of an automatic door sliding along a track. Seo-Yu gasped, stopping for the second time in a minute - not from confusion, but from astonishment.

Working electricity was rare, and Seo was witnessing a miracle.

Chapter Two

The Sun was going down earlier and earlier every day. Hakim and Joel Reese were part way through their trip into town, and picked up their pace once the sun bid farewell. Best not to stay out late. Light was a great guide for searchers in a delicate place. Pointing a couple of fingers around the block as they speed-walked, they decided targeting a CVS pharmacy was the best opportunity.

Hakim walked in front of Joel, and as he stepped within two feet of the doors, reaching out his hands, prepared to yank them apart, there rang out a typical "ding dong". The ding dong emanated from speakers, somewhere on the ceiling in the dim space. The doors slid open on their own. The doors were automatic and working. Hakim turned halfway back to Joel, who shrugged, neither brother trading words for the sake of keeping a low profile, even if the doors already announced their presence to any others.

That was important. The fact that they worked as if things never went downhill in the first place was a nice surprise. The store indicated the opposite of a working condition on the inside, looking like a garment that was aged out of use by a minimum of five years. That was still the best presentation the two brothers could hope for. Better than ransacked.

They were looking for medication, which was a dicey commodity to find in this day and age. People of any background went for that first, whether it be the antibacterial, inhalers, or harder drugs, opioids included. To find any unused or untouched was luck granted. There was a noticeable commotion in the far corner, but shelves obscured their view. That noise could only be from infected people, doing something enticing enough to keep their attention trained away.

No sane people would dare mess around like that. Whatever they were doing, Hakim and Joel minded their own business, and hoped for the same treatment in return. They could not lean on that hope, but they survived so far with plenty of gall left over for runs like these. The brothers, along with their family, understood that they were some of the lucky ones. They lived out of the way in the first place, and had to travel a while to get their supplies, but Hakim and Joel made the journey out every week.

The oldest brother jumped and caught his breath at a shuffling sound, brain trained to think about the infected people that were in a perpetual search for them. A perpetual search for living people, in general. The infected might become alert at the smallest of sounds. A constant high alert on both sides was a requirement. They heard another stir and a couple of flat bangs; an unknown somebody was hitting something against another object at speed.

The infected stayed where they were, focused on whatever happened. They were quiet, opposite what the brothers would expect from a sound like that. The so-far unnoticed men moved forward, sticking to the wall of the store closest to the entrance, and opposite of the infected. They were slow, and as they crossed the store, they held their backpacks against their stomachs, to prevent any noisy jostling.

This was not the first time they ran this gauntlet. Holding backpacks secure was a step they learned weeks ago. The Reese brothers reached the pharmacy counter in a stressed, but overall safe manner. Joel followed his older brother around the counter, both men as cautious as they could manage. There was a swinging door that separated the medicinal portion of the pharmacy from the customer service side.

The counter and see-through plastic shield behind the register were the only other things provided to block off the rest of the store. The flimsy material was what they could depend upon to defend from groping hands and gnashing teeth. A light push and a lingering hand to help keep the door from swinging and slamming and squeaking back and forth, and the boys were in. "Looks like we'll find some things,"

Hakim commented, voice one notch above a whisper. There were some products strewn about the floor, but nothing that acted as a deterrent to the new investigators.

Hakim received no direct response from Joel, but he knew his brother understood. Joel was farther down the line, crouched over a part of the counter, looking at what there was available. Hakim assumed his own search. "Shit!"

Joel's exclamation came at the very moment Hakim turned around to take a visual inventory of possible tasks available. The outcry was too abrupt for Hakim to ignore and keep searching. Hakim flipped his head back to Joel, catching sight of him against the far counter. The cupboard door swung closed. Hakim whisper-yelled at his brother, once he shook off his initial body stammer.

"Joel, what the hell!" Hakim knew he and Joel could not be the only ones in the store startled by the sudden noise. In most cases, the men would retreat to safety or the outdoors, but they did not yet, because of Joel's lack of movement. Hakim watched as Joel's shock wore off, and he gestured at the below-the-counter cupboard, taking a step back as Hakim traded him spots. Hakim gifted Joel one of his staple glares, before bending down to match the height of the little door.

The door was low to the ground, but easy to pull open. Like the bigger one that led into the pharmacy, it swung closed when not held ajar. The entire pharmaceutical area was uniform in that way. Hakim let his eyes adjust to the lack of lighting, focusing on what was inside. On what scared the shit out of Joel.

A little blood is not enough to make Joel react like that... Joel waited until Hakim saw what he saw, before saying anything. Only some of the lights in the store were functioning, setting Hakim's reaction time in the dim behind by a few seconds too long. Hakim wished his hand had not been so close. Joel could almost see the expression on his brother's face, when he saw the same body he did.

"That body startled me! They're not usually hidden like that! Like, what the hell happened there?" Joel's voice was rough upon emergence into the open air. He was still under recovery from when he choked on his own spit.

The two men took a pause and dwelled on the sight of a deceased girl, curled up underneath the counter. Joel was far more on edge, as far as he could see by Hakim's expression, than Hakim was. The dead body was a thorough distraction from their original task. Medicine flipped back to the last priority on either of their minds.

"Maybe she got shot and somebody just hid her, or something. Who cares? We've seen dead bodies before. It's no different just because this one is in a cupboard. Now stay quiet... we've definitely been heard," Hakim scolded Joel, as his mind worked on re-toughening his outer shell.

Joel was too distracted to give a proper response. Hakim saw something else catch his focus - Joel was looking around the room. Hakim had heard a voice, not more than a moment ago, but thought nothing of it. Joel did not pass up the sound. Hakim's ignorance was visible, and he only turned an ear because his brother dwelled on the note.

Joel waved his hands around him in a familiar motion, and the brothers communicated in silence. Hakim's eyes were confirmation to Joel that he had not, in fact, gone insane. The realization reached Hakim, and in that moment, both men were frozen in place. "My God!" Joel breathed out, breaking the silence.

He looked down at the cupboard that held the body. A realization occurred to Joel, right before the same one reached Hakim. They could see the fearful understanding on each other's faces. Joel stuck his fingers in between the little door and the frame, separating the soft wood and taking a peek in, only able to make out the feet of the person in there. There was still no movement, but while paying due attention, her living status was noticeable.

"You're alive?!" Joel felt stupid. He should have known by the first look. Hakim followed along.

"Oh, my, are you hurt? Do you need help?" Then, the strange girl yelled and jerked to the side. The yell startled them.

Then she said a cohesive sentence. "There are two infected near, and they're coming for you!" Both men's attention turned to see over the counter. Lo and behold, she was right. Those infected coming toward them did not have the wits about them to run, but they were there.

Bang, bang. Hakim was the first to take shots at the infected people. Both fell to the floor, knocking over the plastic screens a couple feet in front of them as they did, adding extra drama and raucous to their thuds. The kerfuffle was over, and the store went quiet. Hakim decided to shoot one more bullet into each, for extra security.

Two more bangs. Hakim was not one to take unnecessary risks. "They're dead, dude, stop drawing attention." Joel said. At least his quiet voice made an appearance again. A little late to the game.

"Hey, kid, are there any others coming or was it just those two?" He asked, opening the cupboard door again for courtesy's sake. She would still hear him with the door closed. Hakim was certain there were no more sick people in the store, but she heard what was coming for them before they did, so he did not make too far of an assumption. The girl shook her head, not making any effort to look at him.

Joel joined in, and went back to an earlier topic. "Kid, are you alright? Are you hurt at all?" He was all but stuffing his head into the cupboard, squeezing Hakim against the sharp edge of the intrusive side wall.

If Joel were two feet shorter and 75 pounds lighter, a similar size to that girl, he could fit right next to her in the rectangular space. Joel showed no problem overstepping more than just Hakim's bubble, and as his hand reached in, the girl screamed at the breach of boundaries. She crunched up farther into the back of the cabinet. "Don't touch me!" She screeched, the words coming out in a more coherent way than her first bout of shrieking, but the shock she put the Reese brothers in did not help the reception.

They pulled away for the sake of their ears, and had no problem giving her some space when she showed that kind of urgency. Neither received any more screams, once they backed away. Maybe she did not like strangers. Or adults. Or men.

Whatever the case, Hakim's eyes trailed about the cupboard, and he gasped, as a realization occurred to him. He had caught a glimpse - a glimpse that was quick, but substantial enough - of the girl's face. As asserted before, her appearance in many ways was odd - hell, they thought she was dead, at first! But the strange girl was not healthy, at all.

They could only see a portion of her at first sight, but once Hakim saw her eyes, he *saw.*

The pupils were far dilated, making the irises black as night, like the other infected. Very little white surrounded them. "Shit! Joel, she's been infected!"

"She's infected!? Oh my God! You didn't touch her, did you?!" Joel could not stop himself fast enough from yelling at his brother, in the midst of his fear-ridden panic. Joel knew he did not touch her, so he was safe, but he could not say the same for Hakim.

Hakim let the cupboard door swing closed. Joel stood a few feet back, leaning closer to the door out of the pharmacy. "No, I didn't," Hakim said, as he reached down for the rectangular door again. The way he had to bend to reach the cupboard exacerbated his back pain, but he pushed through. He reached back for his gun at the same time.

The oldest Reese prefaced the killing with a few words. "Sorry about this, girlie. It'll be quick, I promise." Hakim pulled the cupboard door open, slower than the other times, nervous that she would beat him to the punch. *She has to know what is going on.*

She had to, by now. This moment was deadly for either one of them. Hakim forced himself to let a big breath out of his lungs. He had not breathed for too long. The door was all the way open.

The time was here. And she was not revealing an aggressive side. As Hakim Reese approached the moment where he needed to give her the same fate as her counterparts a countertop away, he heard a pitiful whine. As one second after another passed, her voice came back, starting a few last words before Hakim had the chance to flick the safety off of his weapon.

"No, no, no, please don't kill me. Please! I'm not going to hurt anyone. I promise!" Her plea was pitiful.

Though only a whine, Hakim did not have to put in any extra effort to hear it. He figured closure was not unreasonable for such a young victim. He pulled together a reasoning for his argument. His new plan involved the next step to pull the trigger. Hakim flicked back the safety.

The click was the most noticeable part, pre-release of the bullet. "I'm sorry. Even if I don't shoot, in a few days you'll be too far gone, you'll kill a bunch more people, and then die in a week or two. That'll hurt more than this will, so just be glad you can have your last moments with your mind intact." The girl did not say anything back.

Hakim figured as much, but... he did not fire his shot. Something was off-putting about that silence. Some invisible thing - a thought - told him *not* to pull. Hakim's finger twitched, telling him he was hesitating, both in mind and body. The hesitation took too much time.

A petite hand shot up the height of the cupboard, aiming straight at the gun. There was a smack as she shoved the death-dealing weapon up and away from her head, pushing it against the cork ceiling. Hakim could not yank the gun away fast enough, and struggled to take it back once she had a hold. Her palm was on the barrel of the gun, locked in after a heart-stopping moment of fumbling. Hakim tried being more aggressive when yanking the gun away, and she grunted, bringing her other hand up, too.

Hakim had not let go of the gun, as he was not about to lose his weapon to somebody who could kill him with her bare hands, but he could no longer aim the gun at her head. While Hakim was in the process of gaining leverage, she spoke. Her tone held a plethora of urgency.

"Don't touch that! I've already been blind for two weeks! If I was going to lose my mind, it'd be gone by now!" Joel's stammer was equal to Hakim's halted brain processes.

"Two weeks, my god… are you… are you for real? Penelope lost it after only two days,"

Joel finally spit out, more out of shock, than in posing a question. Now directed to Hakim, "Do you think...?" he did not clear up the inference out loud, but the adults had a silent conversation between each other. Two pairs of active eyes conveyed a lot of information. Together, they reached the same conclusion.

Joel groaned and stomped off in the same way a teenager would when a parent told them to go do their chores. Once he was out of sight, Hakim opened the cupboard door, cautious enough to not come so close to the Perdita victim as to trigger another scream. "What's your name?" Hakim was purposeful in his tone, but still came across as kind and agreeable. He did not feel concerned enough in the moment to whisper.

Considering he killed off the other dead in the store, this was one moment Hakim did not feel the need to keep his volume low. He would treasure the moment. The teenager started talking, seeming on a similar level of comfort, even if hesitant. "My name's Seo, for short." She mumbled her words out, and curled up at the same time, hands sinking away into her long sleeved jacket.

Seo's dirty white shoes prevented her feet from disintegrating altogether. Hakim pushed for more info. "And Seo's short for what?"

"Seo-Yu."

"Seo-Yu," Hakim repeated, nodding along with the sound.

"Lee."

"Okay, Seo-Yu Lee?" A nod from her.
"Seo. That is a cool name. My name is Hakim Reese, just so you know."

"The other guy was Joel - he's my brother." Hakim tossed a thumb over his shoulder, and started on a new topic. "We were just in the area, you know… we got things to do…" Hakim was on a stalling tangent. "We want to help you out here, *if* you won't hurt us. Do you have any weapons on you?"

Hakim squatted at the cupboard, still calm as a ladybug on a leaf. "No," was Seo-Yu Lee's answer.

"Okay. How has that worked out for you so far?"

"The infected leave me alone, and I can just keep hiding from other humans. I just need my backpack, and then I can go back home." Seo-Yu sounded like she was crying. Hakim left that topic alone. She did not move to leave the cupboard, to get her backpack.

Hakim took that latency as a cue to grab it for her. He took a second to look around the place, and found the small black and brown thing of terrible quality sitting on the far side of a pharmacy rack. Neither brother pointed it out earlier. There was no reason to focus on something that was not relevant to their search. The bag was quite used, and not what they were looking for.

In all realness, the backpack did not need to be nice. Hakim's face scrunched up at another reminder of the state of things. *No need to care about expensive equipment, these days.* Hakim sat the bag down next to the door with Seo behind, ready for retrieval, once the girl came out. Joel was back in view by the time Hakim straightened his back.

"Hey, this is Seo-" Hakim pointed down, but did not continue, as Joel took a step over to the counter, his hip leaning against the sharp edge of the linoleum. He had something to say. Declining to use his vocal chords, he tapped out some words, with the aim that only Hakim would understand him. No need for the prying, unfamiliar ears to hear what was on his mind. Seo-Yu did not make any suspicions known, but the boys had to stand on the side of suspicion, for the sake of safety.

After a few seconds of their silent word trading, there was a scrape. Heads turned to see the girl brave sliding out of the cupboard. Their word trading stopped, eyes trained. Seo snatched up the straps of the bag and pulled it close to her chest. She did not say anything, just sat on the edge of the floor of the cupboard, hunched.

Seo-Yu's feet tapped on the hairy floor mat. She was antsy. The fact that Seo did not look around or care to see things around her was unnerving. Creepy. *She isn't dead somehow,* Joel tapped out as a final comment.

He may as well have said the words out loud, with how telling his facial expression was. Clapping a hand on the counter after finishing his sentence, he broke the uncomfortable silence that centered over the fact that blind people were not common. Neither brother was used to seeing them.

"Good. You're a smart girl to have survived this long. If you're right about yourself, then you're going to be okay," Joel reassured Seo-Yu, his voice as calm as ever. All of a sudden, the door of the pharmacy slammed against the wall, interrupting the mood of the setting. The brothers set eyes on a new individual.

The younger of the two cussed up a hailstorm as he jumped a surprising distance away. A third mentally-gone infected person decided to join the party. There was little hesitation from Hakim. He put a bullet in that one first, again. As always.

Joel almost rolled his eyes, but he refrained. His brother's eyes were back on him. This one death added more on top of a bigger number, when looking at the grand scheme of things. Joel seemed to have a gun only for back up's sake. He never saw a day when Hakim would not use Joel's as an extra clip, or grab it out of his hands and start shooting, before Joel could start fighting on his own.

"Didn't hear that one?" Joel's comment was in reference to Seo-Yu, and she took a second to answer. He stood around, awkward.

"No." She shook her head, too.

"Let's just get out of here," Hakim said, sounding more like a demand than a recommendation. They were spending too much time in one place. He gestured to Joel and Seo, but realized that hand movements were meant for seeing, not hearing. She provided no response. He back tracked.

"Uh… you can hear when we're walking, right?" He asked.

"Pretty well," she said.

"Okay. Let's stay quiet besides that… I know you know the drill. Save us some of our bullets."

"Okay," she replied. They got on the move.

Chapter Three

Seo felt something from out of nowhere bounce onto her thigh. It was a thing that was round and the same size as her fist, which made her jump in her seat, barely catching the ball-ish thing. The ball was soft. *Cloth.* As Seo-Yu's thumbs felt it out, she realized she was holding a pair of gloves, one folded over the other.

Seo sat up all the way and opened up the pair, flattening them onto her palm. She felt out the fingers, slipping one glove on each hand. They were of cotton, and seemed to be a basic style. Seo-Yu knew the kind; they had a high possibility of unraveling, farther down the road. Not too fine.

She wiggled her wrist, feeling that they were a bit too big for her hands, but they were some kind of warmth for cold fingers. Seo kept them on. The truck, van, big car, or whatever it was they rode in on hummed along. The road was smooth, but there were many twists and turns which threw her orientation for a twist. Not that she knew the area they were going to, anyway.

There was no way they were inside of the city. Enoch was north, but they could not be headed there. There was nothing of value. The canyons were not far, but cars could not drive well in them. Cedar City was tiny, with empty land for miles around.

She could only wonder where they were all headed. Most of Seo-Yu's stuff was back at the apartment, and she had never given the men directions to get there. Even before Seo's ears zoned in, she could tell people in the front seat were muttering between each other. Joel's voice was one of the two, so Hakim had to be the other. But there were three people in the vehicle other than Seo-Yu.

"I still think…" Joel mumbled, but did not finish his sentence. She would have heard more words if he continued. Some kind of emotion took over, instead. Neither of the voices were saying anything anymore. One of them tapped some plastic surface, in a loud enough way for Seo-Yu to hear.

Almost like in the pharmacy, when they did the same on the countertop. A methodic sound. There had to be a pattern. Small conversation continued through words, after that tapping was over. The truck came to a final stop, the engine turning off, key scraping as it left the ignition.

The front pair of doors opened wide. The closed windows kept out so much wind and air that Seo forgot about the season. Somebody, most likely that Hakim guy, came too close to her. He did not say anything to warn Seo-Yu he was there, but by the rustling, he was trying to hand her the backpack. Seo almost touched him in the heat of the bag transfer, and she jumped away in surprise, bag dropping to the floor and her head and shoulder banging into the side wall.

"Oh, shoot, are you okay!?" Hakim raised the question, but Seo-Yu could tell he wanted to keep his distance. There was no rushing to make sure she was not bleeding out, or that there was not a dent in her head. Seo rubbed the crown of her skull, pushing the butt of her hand against her head, the pressure distracting her from what she just did.

"Yeah, I'm alive," Seo-Yu said, as she tried to ignore the inner want to cry.

"Okay. Let's get out the right way, then." The process of getting out of the truck was still awkward the second time around. Nobody could lead Seo out by hand, and there were plenty of "oh"'s and "um"'s while she felt her way to the open doors. Seo-Yu finally hopped off the ledge, landing on loose gravel.

A little bit more talking, all about random stuff. One of the three shoved a length of rope into her hand, and as the rope grew taut, she followed behind. "Are those owls?" Seo asked. She could swear she was hearing owls.

"Yeah, somewhere," Joel responded. *That's cool.* Seo shrugged, and made her actual response out loud.

"Cool. Never actually seen one." Seo-Yu could tell the following silence was awkward. Now, she would never be able to see one. One day, Seo would look back (mentally) and find it funny that no one had anything to say about the issue.

For now, she was acting awkward, too. "Stop," instructed the third voice, which had spoken little up until that moment. The rope lost its tension as everybody holding on in front of her slowed down, and she heard a heavy door scrape open. They filed into some kind of shelter. A cabin, by the sound of the floorboards.

Every step creaked. The insulation was poor in comparison to a commercial-build apartment building, but with some measures, the place may feel cozy. "Charlotte, we're home!" Joel called. *Who is Charlotte?*

The voice of Charlotte greeted them back - not with a hello, but with orders. "Joel, Hakim, Mason... How about you take that stuff and put it away, and then help me out with this." Mason was a second new name. The woman's voice grew closer... and then the energy changed. Sudden, angry yelling ensued.

There was a verbal fight going on, and Seo-Yu did not know where to go. All she knew was that her anxiety was set off. The overwhelmed stranger could not process the situation through all the yelling. She stepped backwards, looking around for anything to help, as if she could see her surroundings. Instinct.

The lady was coming closer. Any second now, and Seo-Yu would be hit with a flying fist. It must have been her eyes that set her off. The voice did not lighten up, even if Seo did not end up beaten to a pulp.

"Oh my god! What the Hell! Why did you bring one of those infected freaks home!? Shoot it, like the animal it is! What the hell do you boys think you are doing!?"

Something was thrown, bouncing a couple times on top of the hard flooring. The situation was physical. The lady screamed and screamed profanities, not stopping until after Hakim tried multiple times to provide an explanation of what was going on.

"This is Seo-Yu Lee, she's immune. She is blind, and the infection stopped at her eyes. Seo's been infected for over two weeks and her mind *isn't* gone." This new information didn't seem to offer any solace to Charlotte.

"I don't care! Take that freak out into the woods and shoot it! Or, bludgeon it with a shovel, I don't care! Just KILL IT!" She was audibly at a breaking point.

"She's just... a normal little girl," Hakim had a level of calm as he tried to explain, but was cut off from further exposition. Charlotte clearly had tears in her eyes, but her voice never broke free of a screech. With such venom, volume, and vitriol, Seo-Yu almost turned and fled to the woods on her own. Seo started to back away, hands reached out behind her, but could not find the door handle. Seo-Yu felt a hand on her arm, which was enough intervention to give her a heart attack.

Barely avoiding an onslaught of death-dealing cardiac arrest, the hand pulled Seo away from the danger of the crying woman. She was so stunned that somebody touched her, that the frozen mindset prevented her from speaking. Seo-Yu's thoughts moved like drying molasses. She was wearing short sleeves. Seo's skin was making contact with their skin.

Then the next thought. That might be them dead, by her own hand. Or rather, by their hand, which would not let go of Seo-Yu's arm, even after a yank. Whoever the arm holder was (she was certain it was an adult man - it was rare that a woman's hands felt calloused) guided her around the side of the cabin. By the sound of

a doorknob and a different kind of creaking -
plastic, maybe?

They were at what Seo could only assume was a shed. Or maybe some other side portion of the house. The person who took her was not descriptive of where they were going. Seo-Yu almost tripped on a threshold. *Yeah, a shed. Or maybe a corn crib fit for a cliché quarantine before they old-yeller her.*

On second thought, it's definitely one of those trailer-transportable sheds. I wonder how easy this glorified box is to lift. The place was cold and not as inviting as an actual out-building would be. Charlotte's yells could still be heard, though dulled. They were not far away, and that was a loud woman.

"I'm sorry about that, sweets. Don't tell Joel, but I'm not a fan of Charlotte either. She bulldozes him, the poor guy."

"You touched me," Seo-Yu said, failing to acknowledge Hakim's lengthy apology.

"I guess you're right. I'll go clean my hands. You'll probably have to stay in here for a while," Hakim said, an apologetic twinge entering his voice on the last sentence. Hakim was now closing the door of this place he confined her to, as soon as he finished. A squeak and a click.

He was gone. Seo felt cold. She sat around for a while, trying to spite the temperature. There was no good way to pick a fight with an inanimate, abstract concept like the cold. There was nothing to do.

Seo-Yu wished that she could read a book, or do the typical boredom wants. There was nothing to accomplish in the night, which was as indistinguishable from day as the color black from dark brown, not that she could distinguish those anymore either.

"Nobody cares," Joel scolded, his voice overall controlled, but he left a hint of venom layered in for indulgence's sake. "We're not going to kill a little girl again." His equally tall, stick-like wife was so angry she growled at him. Char was not going to get her way, and was without a retort, finally. She went off to cook.

They could only hope no food burned while she was out, but even with the best cook in the house back on the job, angry food never turned out a good result. Hakim was back inside, Joel gave him a nod in acknowledgement, and both went to the kitchen out of instinct. Through the open doorway, the aura changed. The average-size kitchen was a tense place. Many knives available to use for stabbing, but with some luck, they could expect no more sour moods to join in the mix, and no more fights to go down.

Chapter Four

"I live here with Joel and his wife, Charlotte, along with their son Mason, and my other niece and nephew, Evie and Sawyer. Um… their parents aren't…" Hakim sighed, stopping his explanation of the family. It sounded touchy. He was not ready to talk about that subject. Hakim's voice was quiet and melancholy, and Seo had to stop herself from putting her hand on his shoulder in a typical gesture of comfort.

Better not risk his life more. Changing direction, he replaced the lump in his throat with a cheery sound. "There's plenty of room for you to stay around for a while, even if there are a lot of us running around the house. Don't worry, you'll be safe in here." *In the shed. There's no safer feeling, I'm sure of it.*

That was where Seo-Yu was at in life. *Some family's empty shed.* The teenager was not acclimated to other people before she was infected, and things hadn't exactly improved.

She was not sure what else to say. After a moment of thinking, Seo worked up a few words. She was not willing to leave the shed empty of sound, after realizing Hakim was done talking.

"I can just be glad to have a place to stay," Seo-Yu mumbled. She was near choking on that sentence. Comparing a lonely life with no one around to a lonely life with others around was a strange mirroring. The two were still overtaken by silence, in the cold but appropriately sheltered area. Hakim sighed.

"Okay. Well, here you go." He handed a stack of something over, heavy but not dense. Apparently he had brought thick blankets for Seo-Yu. She broke a smile as she discovered what they were.

Seo wrapped herself up in them, and for the first time in too long, she was not any colder than she needed to be. Seo-Yu started to space out, ears traveling over to the cabin. She could hear the slight but present sounds of children playing a game, and in the ground, irrigation lines with water dribbling through them. Seo had never seen any of that upon arrival, but hearing showcased everything to her, clear as day. Seo-Yu's thoughts muddled together, creating the onset of a series of sleeping, waking up, eating, trying not to be seen by Charlotte to save her well-being.

Day one, two, three, as many as Seo could put in line in her own mind passed, before Charlotte stopped demanding that someone take her out to the woods and shoot her. That was a special day. Less alienation of the one person not related to the Reese family. There was no more treatment like a rabid dog. More like a strange and unpredictable animal.

Charlotte, called "Char" on occasion by the adults, refused to talk more than needed when she was in the same room, and only referred to her as 'it' when the topic came up. Things were a step up from before, though. It was during dinner that most of the family was in the kitchen, enjoying their time together. Usually Seo-Yu stayed out, but this time she edged around them, hoping she did not interrupt anything as she went for the fridge, where she had left a cup of milk. Seo opened the door, hand following the edge of one of the plastic grates.

There was a papery tab on this one, which signalled her designated belongings. Family members only touched that stuff after Seo-Yu used them. They cleaned them and the dishes went right back. She took out the glass, too which there was a gasp, and a second after a clatter, a beat of stunned silence, and then a smash rang out. The raucous stunned Seo, and she freaked out inwardly, trying to move out of the way, but only managed to crunch down on glass shards.

Charlotte's gasp opened the floodgates otherwise known as her vocal chords. "That girl is still an animal. We're lucky that she isn't so feral anymore." Her voice held an odd sound. That was unexpected.

Was it satisfaction? Accomplishment? *Is she high and mighty about me breaking a glass?* Charlotte did not mind being so rude, even when Seo-Yu was around. There was little push back, because the blind girl and the other diners knew better than to start an argument.

She shook her shoes free of any glass, before putting her tail between her legs and slinking back to the shed. There were many tears, once Seo ensured she was out of sight. Hakim came to the shed, late enough for dinner to be over. He tried to console Seo-Yu. She ignored him enough to make him realize his shaky conversation was not working out the way he wanted.

All Seo could do, anyways, was think of all the things she could not change. "I don't think I want to be here," Seo-Yu said, before Hakim left entirely. That was a true thought, and the sentiment did not relinquish after he left.

Joel and Hakim were ready to make their leave. They did not talk directly to Seo, but with her ear pressed to the wall, she heard them outside the shed, speaking to Charlotte. They told her where they were off to, mentioning streets Seo-Yu was familiar with, all on the edge of Cedar City. Out to get a set of tools for back up - they had run out of something. The name of the thing was unclear.

Doors slammed shut. The truck engine turned over, and the vehicle sped off. Joel's wife resigned herself back into the warmth of the house, that door closing in a less forceful way. Seo-Yu Lee looked around the shed, to no avail. This was one occasion where she forgot that she was not just in a dark room; there was no way for her to see.

Seo-Yu reached down for her backpack. Seo never forgot what was in there. She had no problem remembering what the bag looked like. Black with stylistic brown patches. Those were peeling off the last time she checked.

Two of the zippers were broken, and only the main portion had the ability to latch shut. Of the various places, that was the only one where Seo-Yu put anything, because of the working zippers. She would pick up a new one if she could find one, but turns out that backpacks were a hot commodity during the end of the world. Seo flicked on the lighter for a second. She held down the trigger to keep the little flame alive.

Seo-Yu felt the fire, almost burning her finger with the satisfaction of feeling.

What. Seo-Yu Lee froze when she realized what ran through her head. *I've been through this before. But just with myself.* That was back when Seo-Yu was living on her own.

Breathing curbed, fingers clenching down on the railing of the porch stairs. There were fewer temptations here. *So why again?*

Unsolicited, the thought arrived again, pressuring Seo. *Touch.*

You will get more of the heat that way. I need it to survive. Or else. She was surviving fine before. This was the first time an intrusive thought occurred to Seo-Yu in two weeks.

Why is this happening? Seo wasn't sure how much time had passed, but Hakim had entered the shed startling her. Seo was too disturbed with her thoughts to say anything. "I got this stuff set up for you," he said.

"What stuff?" Seo-Yu inquired back. Hakim was careful to only grab the surface area on top of her leather glove, and he brought her hand over to place her fingers on a string. Seo felt the string out. Before he explained, she could only speculate on why it connected to stakes sticking out of the ground.

"That marks which line is which," Hakim said about the string. With the information, Seo-Yu started to learn which plants in the garden were food, organized by location.

In the same time frame, Seo-Yu found that Hakim was all about improvement - like when he tampered work gloves to fit her better. That substitute was a step higher on the ladder than the cheap pair Seo wore before. She was grateful for the motions like that, and her gratitude increased as Hakim was the only one who was not scared of her. Joel tried to hide his own caution, but it was clear he made sure to keep his distance in any situation involving Seo-Yu.

The same went for the other people in the house, the main reason being serious orders from the parents. She tried not to mind, and was content with the light load company-wise, even if the current quality of the living situation was lower than it was two months ago. Seo was more than happy to have someone to talk to on a consistent basis, for the first time in a long time. She and Hakim were quiet people when there was nothing important to talk about, and they seemed to be content in each other's company, but sometimes held conversation.

Staying on that schedule was all Seo-Yu needed to stay content.

"Do you have any family, kid?" The question came on a day where she sat on a flimsy lawn chair, while he picked from the line of carrots close by, in the garden. Seo shrugged in response. She figured he could see her movements, but followed up with an explanation.

"I don't know. My parents were out of the country when everything went out the window. I'm not sure if they're still alive. I doubt it." Seo-Yu was despondent in voice.

She had not thought of her parents in a long time, and avoided thinking about them during her time spent without them. They were both in their fifties, and neither were very strong physically. All they had was some money. Seo could not count on finding them again.

"I'm sorry, kiddo. They shouldn't have left you by yourself." Hakim had to know how poor of a comfort he was. Then again, she supposed neither of them were any good at comforting the other, so she did not give him flack for trying.

"You don't have to call me 'kid', I'm seventeen." Seo-Yu realized what slipped out of her mouth, and she stopped and considered her age, inwardly. *I'm not sure what I look like now, but I definitely didn't look my age before being infected. Then again I doubt I got taller, so how much could things change?* Hakim let out a gruff laugh, and patted her on the shoulder.

"Whatever you say, kiddo," came his attempt to keep the mood light, even if he never stopped calling Seo the same nicknames over and over. She chuckled, and the two went their separate ways. It just so happened that conversation was absent for the rest of the day. In what felt like moments after Seo-Yu went to bed, scrunched up against the wall of the shed at the side of the house in the forest, she awoke.

Seo awoke to a sudden lack of background noise. She had no clue what the time was, but one sound was gone. How long has that been off? Seo-Yu never thought about how she had become used to that noise over the last two weeks. The sound of water flowing was gone.

Admittedly, there was more noise Seo fell asleep to every night, but the lack of the most monotonous one was jarring. One thing she had not learned yet was how the water pipes on the property worked, but she knew that stoppage of the flow was a bad sign. Seo-Yu waited to see if the water started up again. Maybe it would just last a moment. Without a clock to show her the time, she could not tell how long she waited.

Nonetheless, too much time passed where wind was the only sound. *Yep, that's a problem.* Seo jumped up and did her best to dodge previously memorized obstacles, while running to the cabin proper. Up the stairs and to the locked door, she slammed her palm on the dense wood, over and over.

"Guys! I think there's a problem!" Seo yelled, until the lock disarmed. It took some persistence. Charlotte was the one to answer.

She shouted when she saw who was at the doorstep. "Hakim! Hakim! Your freak is at the doorstep! The wretched freak has gone *feral*!"

Charlotte screamed, walking a few steps away, and waking up everyone else in the house with no cares in the world. Hakim came to heed his summons, his voice laced with worry. "Seo, what's up? Are you alright?" He asked.

"The water pipes! I- I can't hear them anymore. Something's wrong! Something-" her flustered self could not be helpful to the people at the door. Everyone must have been confused when Seo-Yu said this, no doubt giving her weird looks.

"You woke us up because you can't hear any water?" Joel was there, his voice tired.

Groggy. The disruption annoyed him more than the problem at hand.

"They're broken. Something's wrong," Seo repeated, voice shaking. She felt wind as someone ran past her. Either Hakim or Joel trampled down the porch steps. Seo-Yu heard the loud handle of the pump creak as it was pushed down and pulled up, but did not hear any water spill out of the spout like it was supposed to.

"Shit, shit, shit!" Hakim cursed, forcing the handle up and down a few more times, rattling it from side to side, and slapping the thick metal in an attempt to get water out. No matter how much he growled, there was no positive result. Seo heard something crack, and Hakim screamed out in frustration.

Somebody else passed her at the door. Hakim ran back, not all the way to the porch. Joel was that person he met halfway. Some frantic planning ensued, between Hakim and Joel. Charlotte was not included - for whatever reason, and to wherever that may be, she was away.

They had a few water reserves and could collect rain to survive, but with a dry environment, the family did not have enough water for crops and people all at the same time. The men walked back to the water pump to scan the irrigation lines, but soon found that in the dark, maintenance was hard. Nothing could be diagnosed until the morning light peaked. Seo went back to bed, full of unease. The morning came, and though she was hidden away in her shelter, she heard the brothers back out in the garden area.

Boy, were they glad they went out for more tools, not long ago. With that preemptive action there was less stress. But, considering they needed pipes and could not start any real fixes until they had proper supplies, some time would still need to be spent in town. Seo-Yu left the shed to visit them, more to get a real update than for the purpose of sociality. Joel left Hakim at the same time she left the shed.

Convenient. "You're breathing heavy, Hakim. Are you alright?" The uncalled for nerves that Seo felt did not disappear after she asked. Hakim took a moment, before he spoke to Seo-Yu.

"I'm fine, kiddo." Her mouth twitched into a slight smile at the nickname, despite a multitude of protests to nicknames besides the shortened versions of her own name. "I'm just a bit tired from everything."

"That's understandable," she said. She wondered what she looked like to outside eyes now, after being able to clean herself up and properly fill her stomach. Seo-Yu's ears acted as guide in taking in the sounds that Hakim was unable to hear as he did his best to further diagnose the pipes. Her mind wondered as she listened. *Hakim almost sees me as part of the family, doesn't he?* Whether or not it was true, Seo certainly found the thought comforting.

Seo wondered about her parents, at times. Back when Seo-Yu told Hakim they were likely not alive, she was not all that upset. Seo worried if that was a problem. Most people would worry. *Did they love me?*

Or... did they take that opportunity and leave me to raise myself...? That was too grossly pervasive of a thought. She stopped herself from pursing it.

"You can have a quick nap," Seo said. She had previously taken one, and was good to go for the rest of the night. Hakim started like an engine turning over, bringing his attention back into the figurative light. His head had wandered off to some place Seo-Yu did not have the ability to see, even if she happened to have the ability to see.

"No, it's alright, we should keep going." Seo frowned at Hakim, feeling displeased at his answer. This was taking a long time, and by her count, the time was late in the night.

"You're excused. Even I can tell how tired you are. You've yawned about three times in the last three minutes, and I don't think you can think straight anymore. Go to sleep for an hour, Hakim, I'll wake you up if anything happens. I promise," she joked, giggling as if a ticking time bomb might appear in front of them as he slept, and she would act as a savior by disarming it before he awoke.

Hakim did not make any more attempts to insist that he was fine and that they should keep on working. He looked like he was starting to understand what state of consciousness he was in. Tiredness was killing Hakim, and if the universe dropped him into a gun fight, he would be too dizzy to shoot straight. Hakim walked over to the shed since it was the closest building at hand and crashed onto the cot that sat in the corner.

Seo had also never listened to someone fall asleep before. Now things felt awkward. *I always notice these things too late.* Despite the awkwardness, Hakim did manage to fall asleep.

Seo covered him with one of the many blankets he'd so kindly brought her.

She paced around the shed, stopping at a cabinet which was not an original part of the place, but screwed up onto the wall after purchase. Seo-Yu dragged her hand down the front, finding the knob on the bottom of the panel, and looked in as if she could see the contents. Seo knew of little inside, anyways. Scrapped receipts and an empty water bottle, and the last item was put in there by her recently. A knife.

The knife was fine edged; one that Hakim gave to Seo-Yu as a method of defense, on the second day staying at the forest retreat. He taught her how to wield the weapon as best he could, but he was no coach. Or maybe he was a great coach, but did not know how to teach blind people. That was one part Seo could give leeway to. Cleaning the weapon was the easy part, but it took a few tries to do the job at first without her almost cutting her finger open.

The blade was already clean, having never been used on anything dirtier than yarn, but Seo made the motion. She liked that motion a lot, but could not explain why it was so therapeutic. Cleaning the knife was no more effective than brandishing it. At best, Seo-Yu could use the small knife to scare people off, maybe get a stab or two in on someone who was within a foot and a half, but knives were no good in a fight. She knew sound well in the first place, but received one more reminder that she could hear things that no one else could hear.

Some people walked around in the family's cabin, two walls away. One of them a kid, surely, but in total: three. Charlotte was the second out of the three. She was always too noticeable. Seo wished Charlotte were like the rest of the family, who were nice or at the very least indifferent.

The door to the cabin opened. *Somebody's leaving the house. I wonder where to.* Seo-Yu did not mean to continue paying attention, but her ears traced the footsteps, which did not last long - and the door to the shed opened. Charlotte was there.

Seo tried to hide the knife, knowing that holding it wouldn't be a good look for her to the person who hated her most of all. Charlotte noticed her there, and she stuttered for the first time that Seo-Yu had ever heard. The thought never occurred to her that Charlotte could have less than a full cup of confidence. "Oh, I… I, uh… I just needed to see if you knew where Hakim was, but I guess he's right here!" Hakim stirred, but did not come to consciousness.

The older lady stayed something next to quiet as she shut the door. Charlotte was gone. Seo sighed into the emptiness. "That was a little weird," she muttered, to no one in particular. With that Seo decided to get some sleep to prepare for the next day. Hakim had said they were going hunting while Joel salvaged pipes from a neighboring farmyard.

Chapter Five

"Dad, I'll be fine." Seo proclaimed after Hakim told her she could take some of his blankets if she needed them. Hakim felt his heart twist at the mention of "dad", and Seo did not even seem aware that she used the term.

"Hakim?" Seo-Yu spoke again. *She's probably picking up on a sudden change of breathing, or something like that. She picks up on things like that all the damn time...*

"Whatever you say kiddo," Hakim Reese laid down on the dirty ground, positioning his puffy coat to cushion his head. He looked down and zipped the light sweater up, put his hands in pockets, and ruminated on the word "dad". He tried to relax his mind, as he gave his rifle a quick wipe-down. Hakim was tired, and had not slept in twenty-four hours, but he knew they were running low on meat, so he was holding out to see a doe come out for the evening. They were too far from home to go back for the night anyway, so he figured he'd make the best of the situation if he could stay awake. The night grew darker though, and eventually he couldn't see his own hand in front of his face making any decent shot impossible even if the animal was sniffing his boots.

He sunk down into his jacket. Sleeping like this was not quite the plan, but they would manage. The treetops gave them some protection. Seo was off to the side, squatting under a horde of fluffy blankets, even though the temperature could not be lower than 65 degrees at any given time in the week. Hakim sighed and closed his eyes for the last time that night. He wanted to sleep for as long as nature would allow him.

And as the moon moved through the sky, he learned sleep was not going to be as easy of a task as he'd thought it would. Both Hakim and the teenager seven feet to his right knew that going out into the forest was a risky venture, but they couldn't exactly go to the grocery store anymore. Prey like turkey or deer could be wandering around with less fear of people since they likely don't see many anymore. There were various dangers they could run into. A wolf wasn't a likely encounter where they were, but it wasn't entirely unheard of. Seo-Yu, at least, did not have to worry about getting infected from any wild game. It wasn't clear yet whether animals were affected yet, but it wouldn't be hard to tell if they came across one that was.

Hakim's thoughts on bringing her was that super hearing would come in handy for tracking game. But there was something else that the man hadn't taken into account. Other than being short and skinny, her main disadvantage in the wilderness was that she was blind.

Eyesight was important. *Her eyes may be the reason we haven't found any game yet,* Hakim admitted sadly. *She can't see where she walks, so she ends up stepping on the loudest twigs in the whole forest to make sure every animal knows we're here.* That thought was short as Seo started snoring slightly drawing the attention of Hakim and hopefully nothing else.

Seo's hair grew out so much that it reached her waist, and most days she kept it in a braid or a low-hanging bun. Seo-Yu was pretty in a non-traditional horror movie kind of way. She had a nice smile, with a button nose, and almond eyes that were black as night. That last feature gave her a slightly menacing appearance, but she still seemed too innocent to be truly afraid of. Hakim was far more intimidating. A *protector of the family* type; he was a soldier with six years' experience, prior to the outbreak.

He was off duty when the outbreak hit southern Utah. The sickness wiped out the unwitting, conservative population of half the state. The Reese family hid away as best they could. Hakim was 6'5 and muscular, with dark skin and a few unrequited scars. He kept his brown hair in a buzz cut, and had a face with a natural disposition for seriousness, set with a strong jaw and big, light brown eyes.

The intimidating man was with his family when he first heard the news about what was later known as the Perdita virus. No one thought the virus was that big of a deal at first. There were many jokes and much brushing off of shoulders. That was more than two months ago, and they proved wrong. Three days was the average wait time before people started exhibiting their symptoms.

The first to appear is what seems like a usual cold, nothing worrisome. This symptom confused anybody, even the medical experts. The cold turned into a sensational *coldness*, affecting ones' body enough to require a jacket, and they needed to cuddle a little closer to their loved ones. Then, their eyesight started to fade, slow at first, followed by the ability to feel.

The threat was not an everlasting one; by a month in, infected people starved, and the streets were lined with the dead and dying. The media called it Perdita, which translates to 'lost'. The name was more or less accurate. *Accurate to their mental states.* Some people were proactive enough to make an appointment to see their doctor.

Around that time, their minds started to fade, as well. The victims stopped understanding what was going on around them, and within days their only desire was to feel warmth and stay hydrated. And they were desperate for the contact of others. This symptom made the most sense considering humans are made predominantly of water and better yet our bodies keep it rather warm. Many attributes of the virus went unexplained as the country entered panic mode, the largest question being changes in the skin. Victims' skin hardened to a point that they were harder to kill with typical murder methods.

The people affected by Perdita gained improved hearing, but they never spoke. They wandered around like ghosts, empty until they died of thirst. That way, the virus spread like a wildfire. A simple touch from an infected person was enough to contaminate, and push over enough dominoes to create the next victim. When people realized what the virus did, they panicked.

Some people rushed into the city for supplies, while others who already lived in the city ran to the wilderness to avoid those people, and some tried to flee the country. None of that movement helped. On top of the freak out, there were horrible people who tried to pass on the virus to others, on purpose. Hakim's own sister was one who ran into town for a good purpose - picking up her son and daughter from school. She stopped by the store for a few supplies.

While she did, everyone else in the family stayed at the cabin their parents (or grandparents, depending on the generation they belonged in) owned. It was a safe abode. Penelope quarantined herself as soon as she could separate from her children, and refused to touch anyone or anything, even her kids. That was the right move. In six days Penny lost her vision, and in eight days, she lost her mind.

Hakim was the only one who took the fall to put her out of her misery, but no one else was willing to touch the body and risk tracking an infection. She rotted in the open, for a long time.

Only recently had they rid the cabin of the smell. Hakim's eyes opened. The light was beginning to shine again, interrupting his sleep.

Time to go about the day, which proved long. Seo and Hakim were back home late that night. They only caught birds on their day hunting. The two separated before dinner time. Seo-Yu assumed Hakim and Joel would take care of the fowl, and retreated to her shed.

Chapter Six

Charlotte had tuned out the last couple minutes of words. Her hands followed her mind's direction. Though Char's vision was blurry by rage, she saw how scared Seo looked. There was a shriek, before the pieces of duct tape covered her mouth and nose.

The girl fought, but Charlotte had a high upper hand. She could *see* what she did. Charlotte could not count how many times her arms went up and down, side to side, but that girl was now dead. Charlotte put her ear to her chest, to make sure. Yes, dead.

Good. Charlotte sat back on her legs for a second, relaxing as much as she could, now that the heat of the moment was through. *Damn, that's a lot of blood,* she noticed as her excitement caught up with her eyes. Char had seen lots of chickens through to their end, and some dead bodies. This was level 2.

Ought to get clean… she thought. Charlotte stood up, but before she got too far, another thought occurred. Cleaning herself was not the best first step. What would be best would be getting rid of the biggest piece of evidence. The body.

Char found that bodies were hard to hide. That was not a skill she picked up on as a child. She was learning now. "Let's get that blanket…" Charlotte whispered to herself. She grabbed the long cottony throw, and wrapped the body inside.

Only hair of drain-pipe clogging thickness and thin shoes stuck out the ends. "Okay." Charlotte curled her fingers around the part of the blanket that doubled over, and gritted her teeth through the struggle of dragging and lugging the victim to a nondescript area. Her blood was shit - a gross texture, but more helpful than leaky red drops. Less of a trail, only the occasional clump.

That was nothing out of the ordinary. Char spent quite a while exerting herself. "Good thing nobody's keeping tabs on me. Even if I don't start dinner, somebody else can. Just can't let it be suspicious."

She therapized herself further, while she had the time. Charlotte reached a good spot to stop, whether it be tired arms or a straight-forward decision. A creek of flowing water. Huffing, she dipped her hands in the clear, icy water. Char could only make them clean temporarily, but for the sake of her mindset, she got pieces of blood off.

Switching tasks, Charlotte unrolled the rug. She re-dirtied her hands by pushing the body into the flow of the water. *Ice cold,* she nodded. *Exactly what it deserves. Live in that forever, you goddamn piece of shit.*

Of course the water was not strong enough to sweep the body away - this was, however, an appropriate place to ruin a body. There were plenty of fish that would pick away until there was nothing but bones left. Char almost grabbed the knife in her pocket again, but she passed up the urge. Time was running out. Charlotte's heart rate picked up, and flustered, she walked back to the cabin, trying not to seem so pleased with herself.

Killing someone was not as easy as her brother-in-law made it seem. *That is disturbing.* Char tried not to think about that more. In the shed there were a few more of the blankets. She sorted through them.

One had blood on it. *Hopefully no one notices this missing.* Charlotte stood back up, the stained blanket balled up between her arm and chest. Back out to a discreet part of the land, and Char worked at cutting the blanket into pieces, shredding and spreading in the hopes that it would be hard to trace. She then went back to the shed, grabbed a bucket, and washed her exposed skin off.

Back in the house. A change of clothes was necessary. Charlotte hid the current pants and shirt, to slide into the next load. Knife went on the nightstand. She cleaned her hands and face and hair one last time.

No need to leave any hint of a smell of blood. Char put her hair in a bun so none of her hair let drops fall on the floor, and hurried on to dinner prep. Baked potatoes would be easy enough to pass off as having cooked for part of the time she was gone. Slice, slice, slice, six times over into the side of each potato. *No*, she grabbed 2 more.

Sometimes people wanted an extra, and nobody knew that the girl in the shed was no longer eating. Charlotte needed to keep some semblance of the "normalcy" held up for the past 2 weeks.

The boys came home. She offered to take the baked potato to the shed. No need to raise suspicions. Char stood in the shed for an extra moment - moving too fast might spoil the plot. Back inside, out of the chill.

Chapter Seven

Charlotte awoke off of the couch to a cold rush of air as the front door opened. She turned to look and see Seo come through with Joel and Hakim.

"We've got dinner," the men said almost in unison and they placed freshly cleaned ducks on the counter and began to prepare them for the meal. Charlotte smiled and tried her best to ignore Seo who stood in the corner of the room with a bottle of water and a blank stare.

Dinner didn't take long to prepare, and Charlotte had to shake the overwhelming sense of Deja Vu as she cut up the potatoes. The family ate with no interruptions. Charlotte felt content after the cathartic dream sequence that had ensued. *This is a good night,* she thought as she looked at the girl who was eating separate from everyone else on the porch. "Anybody want to play a game?" She proposed, with a smile taking over her face.

"Okay," Joel said. "What one?"

"Apples to Apples," Evie recommended.

"No! Monopoly, or Clue, or something like that," Mason demanded.

"I like Monopoly," Char agreed.

"That's too hard!" Evie complained.

"You can team up with somebody," Joel reminded her. The little girl pouted, but refrained from throwing fits. "I'll grab the board game."

"Hey, I don't think I brought that in from the last time I played that with Seo," Hakim said, words steering Joel away from the game closet. *Oh my God,* Charlotte's mind screamed.

She felt like she could cry, but kept her composure and began uttering her aggressive whispers, "You let that thing touch the board games. You let that thing touch the same games that my children play! I want it gone, or I want you gone. What's it going to be?"

The room fell silent and everybody's attention turned to Seo who was standing in the doorway seemingly unsurprised by the words that were just spoken, "Don't worry about me, it's okay, I'll go." Those were the only words Seo-Yu Lee spoke before she retreated into the woods. No member of the Reese family protested Charlotte's demand, and they all watched until she was out of sight into the dense trees. Soon after came nightfall.

Charlotte woke up to read a chapter of scripture on Sunday morning. That was always how the Sabbath morning went, though her constant coughing interrupted her ritual. "Are you okay?" Joel asked, dressed and ready for the day, but back in the bedroom.

"I think so, just a frog in my throat." She closed the leather-coated book, but did not get out of bed.

"Is it a wet cough or a dry cough?"

"A wet cough."

"Ah," Joel stopped inquiring.

"Can you bring me some water, or something to drink, when you come back up?" Char asked. "I'm going to stay put for a little while longer." Joel nodded and left. He took a long time to bring back a cup of water.

"Thank you." The cup was near full, but did not help quench her thirst. Joel disappeared again, and Charlotte laid back down. She drifted off to sleep within minutes.

"Hey, let me in bed," Joel was there, shaking Char awake. "Did you sleep through the whole day?"

"I guess I must have," she said, scooting to her half of the bed. As soon as Joel settled in, she wrapped her arms around him. It was not quite winter, but the air was cold and the blanket was not doing it.

"Well, if you're coming down with something, I suppose sleep is probably the best thing for you," Joel smiled and returned the embrace.

Charlotte was up and moving the next day, but she felt sick. Char persevered and cooked meals for the family as she felt the need to fulfill her duty.

Perseverance was the wrong choice. Charlotte was lost, she just didn't know it yet. Before long, the kids went too. Joel was the next one. Hakim was the last to feel the suffering, but soon, the house was empty.

Chapter Eight

Seo put one foot in front of the other clumsily catching weeds and branches as she timidly made her way through the forest. Even in the night time the forest was alive with sound, none of it useful. There was the chirping of various insects that rang through the open spaces and bounced off of every nearby tree. The wind was doing its best to rip every last browning leaf from its stem creating a cacophony of crackles that hid the sound of any potential footsteps around the girl. Seo-Yu was helpless in this environment, and she was just beginning to realize it.

Seo could hear running water up ahead. It had been a few days since she'd been sent away from the Reese family, and she hadn't had anything to drink yet. There was a few ounces of water in the one bottle she had, but she was saving that for desperation. By the sound of the stream ahead her luck was turning around. As the sound grew closer Seo began to move faster. The thirst was more than she could bear.

As she pickup up into a full-on run, her foot was caught on the roots of a nearby tree that had grown too large. She tumbled head first into the coldest water that Seo had ever felt in her life. Despite the unbearable coldness, she still gulped down as much of the water as her stomach could hold. Her thoughts flipped back and forth between only two things; *Cold, Thirsty, Cold, Thirsty, Cold…Oh know, it's finally happening isn't it.*

Seo pulled herself out of the water and stood shivering on the edge of the creek listening to its soothing sounds, flowing with a deceptively deadly rage. She did not bring any blankets with her into exile. She did not know what she was going to do next. Since she had always gone through the effort of crossing the creek, it wouldn't make sense to try and go back, so forward seemed the only reasonable answer.

As she moved on, Seo noticed the sound of the stream fading behind her and something knew replacing it. The sound was strange and melodic. As she grew closer she began to identify the culprit. It was an owl like the one she'd heard when she first arrived with the Reese family. She continued closer and closer to the sound expecting to hear a crash of wings as the creature fled once she got to close. The crashing never came.

Eventually there was a soft cooing that seemed to be coming from directly in front of her. She reached out slowly with one hand and felt the fluff around the creature's neck. It had been a long time since she'd seen a picture of an owl, and Seo was doing her best to remember what they looked like as she gently caressed the animal her hand sinking deep into its coat. *This thing is all feathers isn't it?*

Seo stood there staring ahead, with the creature staring back into her eyes. They had the same black beady eyes. Maybe that's why the raptor wasn't afraid of her. It felt some primitive connection to the infected girl. It suddenly jump up with a flail of its wings and landed on the shoulder of the girl. Seo cried out in shock but also laughed with excitement, although the laughter didn't last long. *I can hear the bird in my ear and its feathers are tickling my neck, but I can't feel its talons.*

Seo was frightened by the loss of sensation she was beginning to feel. She didn't know how much time she had left. The bird was cooing softly in her ear every time she turned her head. It only stopped when she faced a deliberate direction. *It's guiding me? I really am starting to lose my mind.*

Seo walked on and suddenly found herself in a surprising silence. The insects that were ruling the airwaves prior to meeting her new friend were all beginning to fade. The wind had subsided and she was left only with the crunch of leaves under her own steps and the cooing of the owl in her ear.

It wasn't long before Seo walked head first into the object she was being led to. It was a tree. A very dead tree. Seo felt around with her slowly fading senses wondering why she was brought to this object, until she realized that it had a rather large hollow carved into it. It was just big enough that she could crawl in and increase her body temperature enough to maybe survive another night. The owl left her with one swift pump of its wings and returned to its forest home. *That must have been an elaborate hallucination of my dying brain,* she thought despite hearing each flap of the creature's wings as it flew away.

Seo closed her eyes and welcomed what little warmth the tree was able to provide her with. Sleep found her rather quickly. She did not dream, and she did not even notice the passing of time before awakening to a voice.

"Hey girl, are you okay?" came a voice from outside of the hollow. By the sound of the voice Seo gathered it was likely an elderly man. Probably a loner type with a cabin somewhere in the woods. Seo wanted desperately to tell him to go home. She wanted to have the courage to tell him to get far away from her, but she couldn't.

The cold, the thirst, and the loneliness were becoming more than she could tolerate.

"Do you have a gun?" Seo asked as she turned towards the man's voice exposing her eyes.

"Yes." Came an uneasy, reply from the man.

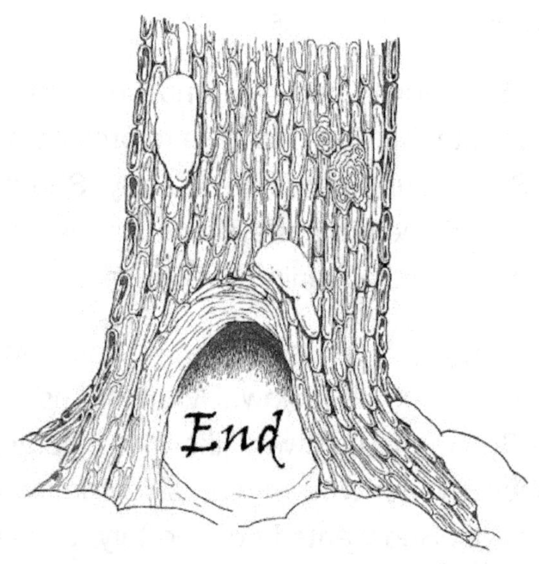

Thank you for reading my story!

There are more available on amazon.

 Also, go ahead and follow me on social media to tell me how much you liked this book! Unless you didn't like it, in which case you should follow my social media so you can tell me how much you didn't like it!

https://linktr.ee/loganeffling

www.ingramcontent.com/pod-product-compliance
Lightning Source LLC
Chambersburg PA
CBHW061538120726
48001CB00004B/1617